SILENT VISITOR

The dog barked insistently. "Boxer, stop!" Bethanne said, but the dog kept on.

"Look!" Mark pointed at the tall fir tree in the corner of the yard. "Someone's standing there," he said.

Bethanne peered at the tree. "It's just the tree's shadow."

Boxer was still barking.

You're being silly, she told herself. There's nothing there. Mark just thought he saw something because of Boxer's barking.

Approaching the tree, Mark pushed aside the long branches. A spicy scent filled the air.

"See anything?"

"Yeah," Mark said, "I do."

He bent to the grass. When he stood, he held a single red silk rose.

Other Avon Flare Books by
Janet E. Gill

WHEN DARKNESS CALLS

FATAL DELIVERY

JANET E. GILL

AN AVON  FLARE BOOK

For Kathleen

FATAL DELIVERY is an original publication of Avon Books. This work has never before appeared in book form.

AVON BOOKS
A division of
The Hearst Corporation
1350 Avenue of the Americas
New York, New York 10019

Copyright © 1996 by Janet E. Gill
Published by arrangement with the author
Library of Congress Catalog Card Number: 96-96545
ISBN: 0-380-78350-9
RL: 6.7

First Avon Flare Printing: November 1996

AVON FLARE TRADEMARK REG. U.S. PAT. OFF. AND IN OTHER COUNTRIES, MARCA REGISTRADA, HECHO EN U.S.A.

Printed in the U.S.A.

RA 10 9 8 7 6 5 4 3 2 1

1

Bethanne took the Saturday morning *Valley Herald* from the front doormat. Moving toward the kitchen, she unfolded the paper. The headline leaped out at her.

ROSEKILLER STRIKES AGAIN!

"Please, please, no," she whispered, gazing down the page to the picture of the killer's third victim. A girl about sixteen—Bethanne's age. Blonde, big smile, pretty as a model. No one Bethanne knew. Her sigh of relief brought immediate guilt. How could she feel good about anyone's death?

But that's not what I meant, she argued.

Continuing to the kitchen, she scanned the article. The girl's parents had moved the sixty miles from Seattle to Valley two months ago. They wanted to escape what they called the "craziness of the city." She had come last week after finishing out the school year in Seattle. Like the previous victims, she'd worked part-time as a model.

Friday night, her dad had dropped her off at Valley's teen club. Kids who remembered her being there said she'd left about eleven, alone.

Since her house was only a short distance away, her parents figured she'd decided to walk home. The killer had struck two blocks from her destination. Just as in the other two murders, he'd used a piece of rope to strangle. And left a long-stemmed silk rose on the body.

Bethanne hadn't known the first murdered girl. She had been from Seattle, visiting her grandparents in Valley over spring break. But the second one went to Ridge High, Valley High's main rival. Bethanne had run against her in two track meets, beating her both times. Briefly, Bethanne felt the girl's handshake, saw her smiling face. This other girl would have been like that, enjoying life, never expecting it to end so suddenly.

It must have been so terrible for them, Bethanne thought, a shiver climbing her back. All at once to realize what was happening.

"Morning, Bethanne," her father said as she entered the kitchen. He sat drinking a cup of coffee at the table.

"Morning, Dad."

He looked at her. "What's the matter?"

She thrust the paper into his outstretched hand. His eyes widened when he looked at the headline.

"Did you know her?" he asked.

"Not this time."

He scanned down the page, his jaw tightening as he read. "This is the third one in less than two months. Why can't Dan catch the guy?"

Dan Reid was Valley's chief of police. He and Bethanne's dad had grown up best friends.

"I'm sure he's trying, Dad," she said.

She poured cornflakes and milk into a bowl and

2

joined her dad. June sunshine spilled through the window beside her, splashed onto the yellow-and-white checked tablecloth. Her dad had buried himself in the paper.

Weird how the day can go on just like normal, she thought.

She shook herself mentally. She had something important to do. She couldn't dwell on the killing.

Taking a bite of cereal, she thumbed through the rest of the newspaper. She pulled out the classified section and turned to the Help Wanted page. School was out, and she was finally old enough to have a real summer job. No more of the waiting-for-someone-to-call baby-sitting. No more five o'clock in the morning paper route. No more pulling weeds for the neighbors. No more working for pennies.

She needed to make good money. The track coach said if she went to the summer training camp at the end of August, she had a good chance of qualifying for the state track meet next year. But the camp was expensive. Her parents said she must earn half the money.

Her dad had offered her a job at his drugstore, but he didn't really need her there. And she wanted to do something on her own.

She ran a finger down the first row of ads. There were jobs at the two fast-food restaurants, but friends had told her sometimes you had to be at work by four in the morning. Or work until midnight. She didn't have a car, and her parents would never agree to her riding her bike in the dark. Especially now, with a killer running around.

Her finger stopped on the next row.

LANDSCAPING *work. Part- and full-time. Good summer jobs for students. 555-7591*

Pulling a pencil from the box on a shelf behind her, she circled the ad. A step up from weeding, she thought.

She liked working outside, and she only wanted to work part-time. The rest of the day she planned to hang out with her friends at Riverfront Park. Her friends—and with any luck, Mark Stabler. She pushed that thought away. If she started dreaming about him, she wouldn't get this done.

Her finger moved down the page.

PART-TIME NANNY *and research assistant. Care for four-year-old, some library work. $7.00/hr. 555-1003*

Seven dollars! Bethanne thought. Four hours a day, five days a week . . .

Quickly, she jotted down the numbers in the margin of the paper. One hundred forty dollars a week! She'd have more than enough for training camp.

But everyone would want that job. What were her chances? Nevertheless, she marked it.

She finished reading the section. No other ads worked for her.

Pulling the phone onto the table, she tapped in the number from the first ad. On the second ring, an answering machine clicked on. A man's voice spoke.

"If you are calling about the landscaping job,

4

leave your name and number after the tone. I'll get back to you."

When the machine beeped, Bethanne said, "This is Bethanne Taylor. My number is—"

"What are you doing?" Her father grabbed the receiver and plunked it down.

"Daddy! I was applying for a job."

"With whom?"

Bethanne pointed to the ad. "The machine said to leave my name and number."

"What company?" he asked.

"He didn't say. What difference does it make? It's a summer job. What are you trying to do?"

He patted her hand. "Sorry, honey. I'm a little jumpy." He leaned across the table toward her, his face serious. "Listen, Bethanne. Leaving your name and number on an answering machine is taking a chance. Especially now. That landscape guy could be the killer. If he has your phone number, he can track you down." He sighed. "While all this is going on, why don't you just work at the drugstore? At least, I'd know where you were."

Her dad was so paranoid. And he was treating her like a little kid. Besides, all three girls killed had been really pretty. Things like that didn't happen to ordinary people like her.

"How do I get a job if I can't leave my name?" she asked.

He looked down the paper. "Try the other one you circled."

She didn't hold out much hope for that one, but she dialed the number. A woman answered.

"This is Bethanne Taylor. I'm calling about your help-wanted ad. I suppose the job is filled."

The woman laughed. "As a matter of fact, it's not. How old are you?"

"Sixteen."

"Do you enjoy children?"

Bethanne had never minded baby-sitting. And she always had fun playing with her two young cousins. "Yeah, I do," she said. "I've had the Red Cross baby-sitting class, too."

"I'd want you from eight to twelve in the morning," the woman said. "Kimmie, my daughter, is in preschool two of those days. That's when the library part comes in. I have a lot of books I want catalogued according to the Dewey decimal system. You'd need to work in the library. Would you be willing to do that?"

"Oh, sure," Bethanne said. She'd liked libraries ever since her mom starting taking her to story-time when she was three.

The woman laughed again. "You'd be surprised at how many people didn't want to do that. Well, why don't you come over, meet Kimmie, and we can talk more about the job? About noon? I'm playing tennis at two."

"Okay," Bethanne said.

"My name is Kristine Kirk. We live in Forest Glen. Do you know where that is?"

Did she! *The* most exclusive area in all of Valley. Large old homes, secluded, built for the farmers and timber men who'd made it big in the town's early days.

After getting directions to the house, Bethanne hung up. Just then, the back door swung open. Her mother, in shorts, tank top, and running shoes, came into the kitchen. Her face gleamed with sweat. A large copper-colored dog trotted behind her. The dog's tongue hung out, and he panted loudly. Going right to Bethanne, he rested his head on her knee.

"Hi, Boxer," she said, hugging him. He was her dog, a birthday gift when she'd turned nine. He'd been the recipient of all the love stored up since she was five. That's when she'd started begging for a baby sister.

Her mother set a bowl of water down for Boxer. He lapped it up noisily. She wiped her face with a towel, then poured herself a glass of water.

"Have to get out earlier on these warm days," she said after drinking it. She glanced at the newspaper on the table. "How's the job hunting?"

Bethanne grinned. "I've got an interview in Forest Glen. Seven dollars an hour for baby-sitting."

Her mother's eyebrows rose. "Those people sure have money to throw around. What family?"

"Last name's Kirk," Bethanne said.

"Ken Kirk?" her dad said. "He's in Rotary. Gave a talk a couple months ago about financial planning."

"They moved here about five years ago," her mom added. She taught seventh grade and was a member of the city council. She knew almost everyone in town and kept up on everything that was going on. "They have a financial advising firm in the Tollefson Building," she added.

Bethanne knew that structure. Everyone did. Built two years ago, it had immediately become a landmark. Its ten stories rose above all the other buildings in town. The main-floor entry was marble. An outside courtyard had fountains and gardens that bloomed even in winter. Only the most important businesses, like Valley Savings and Loan, were located in the Tollefson Building.

"So what do financial advisors do?" Bethanne asked.

Her dad shrugged. "Sell insurance. Help people and businesses choose stocks and bonds. Watch over their investments."

"Do we go to them?" Bethanne asked.

He laughed. "We're not in their league. People who use their service have lots of money—like tens of thousands of dollars. The Kirks take a percentage of the money they handle. They've built quite a business since they started here."

"Looks like you'll be moving up in society," her mom said.

"I haven't even gotten the job," Bethanne said. "But now I'm worried. Should I get all dressed up when I go talk to her?"

"I met her at a council meeting," her mom said. "She's young—late twenties—and seems pretty easygoing. Put on something you'd wear to school."

"And my lucky earring," Bethanne added.

"Definitely," her mom agreed.

Bethanne pulled on a purple T-shirt and white skirt. She combed her hair out, then decided to put it in a single braid. That would make her look more efficient. For the millionth time, she wished her hair were either lighter or darker. It was such a nothing color—dishwater blond.

Yuck, she thought. It was bad enough to have the color. Why did it have to have such a repulsive name?

She put her lucky gold hoop in one ear, two tiny silver fish in the other, then laced up her sneakers.

On her way through the kitchen, she paused by the phone. She was dying to call Peri and Dot and tell them about this job. But then, what if she didn't get it? She'd feel really dumb making up excuses.

Leaving, she shouted good-bye to her mom, in the back weeding the huge vegetable garden. Boxer went with Bethanne to the garage.

As she opened the garage door, a faded red pickup with a dented left fender pulled up in front of her house. Stacks of newspapers filled the bed of the truck. A man in a long black overcoat climbed out and shuffled up the driveway. From under a navy watch cap, his light hair straggled to

9

his shoulders. He needed a shave. Tail wagging, Boxer bounded out to meet him.

"Hi, boy," he said, squatting to pet Boxer.

Bethanne glanced around. In the corner of the garage sat bags of newspapers and aluminum cans. Her dad had forgotten to put them out when he'd left for the drugstore.

"Hi, Birdman," she said when the man reached her.

"Afternoon, missy." As he touched his fore-head, his smile showed perfect white teeth.

Birdman rarely spoke to anyone. Not much was known about him, except that he was a Vietnam War vet. Over the years, Bethanne's mom had shared produce from her garden with him. Once in a while, he talked to her. He'd told her he came from Seattle. His father was a dentist there.

Now, giving Bethanne another bright smile, he picked up two bags of newspapers and carried them out. Boxer bounded after.

Watching Birdman, Bethanne wondered, as she often did, why he always wore that long overcoat and cap. On a day as warm as this one, he had to be burning up.

Returning, Boxer sat by her mom's car. He gazed at her with pleading eyes.

"Oh, Boxer," she said, scratching behind his ears. He loved car rides, and she always felt bad leaving him. "Sorry, fellow, but it's too warm for you to wait in the car. We'll go to the park when I get home."

She gave him a dog biscuit from a bag on a shelf. She'd set the treats there especially for times when she couldn't take him. Tail drooping, he carried the biscuit into the kitchen.

"I'm backing out," Bethanne called to Birdman. He was dropping the papers in the truck. "Wait a minute to get the other stuff."

He stood at the curb while she steered the car to the road. Waving to him, she drove to the corner and turned left at Second Street. Forest Glen was about five miles north of town. At the Forest Glen Golf Course, the road curved. She passed a large clubhouse, then entered a narrow lane lined with evergreen trees and huge rhododendrons. Only mailboxes and gravel driveways suggested houses stood behind all the shrubbery.

She counted the driveways and turned in at the fifth one, as Mrs. Kirk had directed. Passing a tennis court, Bethanne stopped before a three-car garage. It was attached to a wood-and-brick rambler that went on and on.

Wow! she thought. I really want this job.

She checked her face in the rearview mirror. After tucking in a strand of hair, she smoothed her lipstick.

"Relax," she whispered. "It's just a house. They're just people. Act normal."

But would that be good enough?

She took a deep breath, then another.

"Ready, set, go." She touched her lucky earring, then climbed from the car.

The front door opened at her knock. A small solemn-faced girl looked up at Bethanne.

"Are you my baby-sitter?" The child spoke with a slight lisp.

Bethanne smiled down at her. She was adorable. She had a heart-shaped face, corn-silk hair, big blue eyes.

"I hope so," Bethanne said.

11

An attractive auburn-haired woman came up behind the child. The woman wore a white tennis skirt and shirt. "Hi," she said. "You must be Bethanne. I'm Kristine—call me Kris. And this is Kimmie." Kris placed a hand on the little girl's head. "This is Bethanne, Kimmie."

"Hi, Bethanne," Kimmie said.

Inside the house, Bethanne blinked in the dimness. She followed the woman and child past a sunken living room, a dining room, and into a large family room with a brick fireplace. Everywhere were paintings, sculptures, bouquets of flowers.

Kris gestured to a chair. "Sit down. Would you like some lemonade?"

Should I say yes? Bethanne wondered. But her mouth was so dry, she needed something.

"Sure," she said. "Thanks."

"Me, too," Kimmie said. She followed her mother into the kitchen adjacent to the family room.

While Bethanne waited, she gazed out the sliding glass door. A brick and concrete patio surrounded a large swimming pool. Sunshine glinting off the water made her blink.

Kris handed Bethanne a tall glass of lemonade. Bethanne took a sip. The tartness tingled her mouth. She swallowed and felt the cold liquid slide down her throat, pool in her stomach.

"Do you like to swim?" Kris asked.

"Love it," Bethanne said, glancing at the pool again. "My parents started me in swim lessons when I was about Kimmie's age. They worried because of the river being so close."

"Kimmie began lessons last year—for obvious

reasons." Kris gestured to the pool. "She does all right. And she knows not to be around the pool unless someone's with her. Still, there's always a chance something could happen. Ken, my husband, wants someone who can handle an emergency. Of course, I do, too."

"I got my lifeguard's certificate last year," Bethanne told her, "so I know how to handle those problems. Trouble is, I sunburn too easily to be a lifeguard."

"I can relate to that," Kris said, sitting on the couch. "All sunshine means to me is peeling and freckles."

Kimmie stood before Bethanne. "My daddy calls us his fair-skinned beauties," Kimmie lisped.

"I'd say he's right," Bethanne said.

Kimmie turned abruptly and left the room.

Did I say something wrong? Bethanne wondered. Doesn't she like me?

"This summer, I'm working half days Monday, Wednesday, and Friday," Kris said, not seeming to notice Kimmie's departure. "Kimmie's in a day care preschool Tuesday and Thursday. She's gone every day during the year, but Ken thinks children need time to themselves. We decided to let her stay home some this summer. Do you have a car? Some days you'll need one to get to the library."

Bethanne hadn't expected this. But her mom was home all summer. And, if necessary, Bethanne could always drive her dad to the drugstore and use his car.

"That's no problem," she said.

"Good. Let me show you that part of the job."

She led Bethanne to a room down the hall. Bookshelves lined two walls. Against a third, a

13

desk holding a computer stood alongside a printer on a printer table. French doors on the last wall opened onto the patio and pool. Stacks and boxes of books covered the floor and were piled on the shelves.

"These are reference books we use in our business," Kris said. "For our house insurance, we need a list of them. I want you to type the names into the computer. Then take the list to the library and get the catalogue number for each book. We'll arrange them in order on the shelves." She looked directly at Bethanne. "You're not afraid of a computer, are you? One woman who called said she was."

"I took a computer class at school," Bethanne said.

Kimmie entered the room. Face serious, she held out a large, dark-haired baby doll to Bethanne.

"Heather wants you to hold her," Kimmie said.

When Bethanne took the doll, Kris said, "Looks like you've made a hit. Heather doesn't get friendly with everyone."

"What a sweet baby," Bethanne said, handing the doll back to Kimmie. Kimmie nodded.

Kris looked at her watch. "It's getting late. I thought Ken would be here by now. He wants to meet you. He has to approve of you, of course. I'm sure he'll think you're just right for the job. That is, if you want it."

Do I want the job? Bethanne tried to control her grin. "I'd love it," she told Kris.

"How's that sound, Kimmie?" Kris asked.

"Heather likes Bethanne," Kimmie told her.

Kris laughed. "I can't argue with Heather. Bethanne, why don't you fill out some papers while we wait for Ken?"

Somebody pinch me, Bethanne thought as she followed Kris and Kimmie to the family room.

Bethanne handed Kris a folded piece of paper. "Here's a list of people I've done baby-sitting for. You can call them to check on me."

"Sure," Kris said, glancing at the list. "Are you related to Jean Taylor on the city council?"

"My mom."

"I met her once. She's very nice."

From a drawer, Kris took a pen and paper. "Fill this out. We'll be hiring you through our company—helps with taxes." She winked at Bethanne. "And where it says job applying for, put 'consultant.'"

Consultant. That sounded better than baby-sitter. And Bethanne didn't care who hired her, as long as she had the job. At the top of the page were the words KIRKS' FINANCIAL CONSULTING. On the lines below, she filled in her name, address, and Social Security number.

As she finished, a man's voice called from the entry.

"That's my daddy," Kimmie said.

Bethanne watched the man enter the family room. Good-looking, medium height with gray-streaked dark hair. He wore a dark business suit and seemed about her dad's age, mid-forties. Kris stood.

"Ken, this is Bethanne Taylor. Her mom's on the city council. Jean Taylor. We met her at that meeting last year. I sort of told Bethanne we'd hire her. I hope that was okay."

Bethanne shifted in the chair, uncomfortable under his stare. Once at the park, she'd seen the same look on a garter snake watching a baby bird.

"Call me Ken," he said so suddenly Bethanne jumped. His voice was deep. His smile was no more than lips parting. It showed shiny teeth, made even whiter in contrast to his dark mustache. "She'll do very nicely," he told Kris.

Do nicely? Bethanne thought. For baby-sitting? What was this guy's problem? And why did his stare make her neck hairs stand on end?

Taking the papers from Bethanne, Kris glanced over them. "I guess that's it," she said. "We'll see you Monday morning."

I liked this job better before I met him, Bethanne thought. I hope he doesn't spend much time at home.

Kimmie took Bethanne's hand. "Can you come to the club with us now?"

"Not today," Bethanne said. "I promised my dog I'd take him to the park."

"You have a dog?" Kimmie said, her eyes widening. "Does he bite?"

Bethanne laughed. She would enjoy this job despite Ken Kirk. "Boxer only bites his dinner," she told Kimmie.

Kimmie frowned. "Why do you call him Boxer?"

"On my birthday, when I was nine years old, I opened a big box. Inside there was this little puppy. So I named him Boxer."

"Will you take me to the park someday?" Kimmie asked. "And Boxer?"

"If it's okay with your mom."

"I'm sure it will be." Kris checked her watch. "We better go." Turning to Kimmie, she said, "Get my racket, honey, will you, while I show Bethanne out?"

"'Bye, Bethanne," Kimmie said and scampered from the room.

At the door, Kris said, "Monday morning, we'll spend time going over everything."

Bethanne floated to the car. Inside, she checked the mirror. That piece of hair had escaped again, but it hadn't mattered. She touched her earring. "Way to go," she said. She touched it again. "Just keep him out of the house when I'm there," she whispered.

She turned the car around and headed toward town. She'd stop by BoTeek, the trendy clothes shop where Peri worked, and tell her what just happened.

Bethanne drove down Second Street, past the turn to her house and on to the town of Valley. The main streets through town, A, B, C, ran east and west. They were north of and parallel to the river. The alphabetical streets crossed First, Second and Third Streets, forming a grid. The simplicity of the design had led to a lot of jokes about the intelligence of Valley's founders. Bethanne liked the arrangement. When she told someone she lived off Second on F Street, they knew right where her house was.

Turning right on B Street, she pulled up in front of BoTeek. In the window hung a modern painting with swirls of bright pink and oranges. Pink and orange flowers lay strewn about. Summer clothes in the same colors were displayed around it. Looking between them, Bethanne could see Peri through the window. Tall, dark haired, beautiful. She was waiting on a customer, so Bethanne stayed in the car. Peri worked partly on commission. Bethanne didn't want to mess up a sale.

Watching her, Bethanne remembered the first time they met, in preschool. Bethanne had never seen black hair or slanted eyes before. She'd been so fascinated, she'd gone home and covered her head with black construction paper. She'd walked around pulling on the corners of her eyes. When her mom asked what she was doing, she said she was stretching her eyes so she'd look like Peri.

Bethanne's mother put her in the car and took her to the library. There her mom showed her books with pictures of people of all colors and face and eye shapes. And then her mom broke the terrible news. Kids looked like their parents. Peri had slanted eyes and black hair because her mother and father did. Bethanne would never have eyes like that.

Just then, Peri's customer carried a large BoTeek bag out of the shop. Bethanne went in.

18

Peri was straightening a row of dresses on the back wall of the small shop. She wore a bright pink jacket and skirt, like one outfit in the window. Sally Martin, the owner, had her model some of the clothes while she worked.

Bethanne pushed through the racks of blouses, jackets, and pants. Most of them, she knew, cost more than she was going to make in a week.

"Hey, Bethanne, you look sharp," Peri said. "What's up?"

"I just got a job." When Bethanne told her about the salary, Peri let out a small shriek. "Just for baby-sitting! Good work."

"No," Bethanne said. "I'm a consultant."

Peri's laugh was low and throaty. "I know Kris Kirk. She shops here a lot. And Kimmie. Real cute kid. Serious, like a little owl. I did get her to smile one day. But, you should know . . ." Peri paused. "No, maybe I shouldn't tell you."

"What?" Bethanne asked. Peri was a worrier. Still, she always had a pretty good sense of what was going on around her. Maybe she knew something about Ken Kirk.

Peri glanced at a door marked EMPLOYEES. "Sally's taking a break back there." She dropped her voice. "I don't think she'd want me to tell you this. You have to promise not to say anything."

Bethanne nodded. With a buildup like that, she would promise almost anything to hear what Peri had to say.

"Kris comes in every month," Peri continued. "She buys like two, three hundred dollars worth of clothes. Sometimes after she leaves, something's missing—a necklace, a scarf. Just little stuff, things I know she can afford."

"You mean she steals things?" That thought didn't go with the woman she'd met that morning. "She seems pretty nice." Bethanne took an aqua sundress from the rack.

"If it happened only once, I might think I'd made a mistake. But it happened two times. And then last week, I knew for sure."

"Why?" Bethanne held the dress to herself and studied her reflection in the mirror.

"We'd just gotten these new earrings in." Peri touched the bright pink hoop earring she was wearing. "I'd put five packages on the rack. Kris was our first customer. She bought a bunch of clothes. When I started to ring them up, I noticed an earring package was gone. I thought she might have taken it and forgotten to tell me." She shrugged. "That happens sometimes. When I asked her if she wanted to buy earrings, she said no. Said she couldn't buy any more or her husband would cancel her charge card. That's when I knew for sure she was stealing." Peri shook her head.

It was hard, and disappointing, for Bethanne to believe Kris Kirk was dishonest and sneaky. But Peri had no reason to make up a story like that.

"Her husband is kind of a creep," Bethanne said. "And I got the feeling he was in charge. She couldn't even hire me without his okay. Why doesn't Sally do something?"

"She said Kris is too good a customer. A twenty, thirty dollar loss isn't much in comparison to what she buys. I don't agree with her. No one should get away with stealing. But it's her shop." Peri frowned. Her eyes met Bethanne's, reflected in the mirror. "I hope this doesn't mean you won't get paid."

"Don't worry," Bethanne said. "I'm on the company payroll." She turned and held the dress's skirt out. "What do you think?"

"Save all your summer paychecks and you can probably afford it," Peri said, laughing.

Just then, Sally came out the employee door. "Hi, Bethanne," she said.

Sally wore a navy blue jumpsuit that made her look even taller than her six feet. Her hair was shiny blond, smooth, chin length. She'd worked as a model in New York City, and on the shop walls hung pictures of herself taken from fashion magazines. When she was too old for the job, she'd returned to Valley, where she'd grown up. She started BoTeek then.

"Bethanne's got a job baby-sitting Kimmie Kirk," Peri told her.

Sally laughed. "That little one, so cute. Watches everything, takes it all in like she's figuring out the secrets of the universe or something."

Peri and Bethanne followed Sally to the front of the shop. Peri stopped at the jewelry counter to hang a gold bead necklace back on the rack.

"Dot called," Peri said to Bethanne. "Wants us to go to a movie tonight. And the Football Four, of course."

Bethanne laughed. "Of course."

The Football Four was the group of four football players, who all had crushes on Dot. They followed her around in a pack, supposedly so no one would get the upper hand.

"The Football Four will drive us," Peri went on.

"They're going to keep watch over Dot until the Rosekiller is caught." She pointed to the morning paper lying by the cash register. "Did you see he got another girl?"

Bethanne nodded.

"She was in the shop on Wednesday," Peri said, "with her mom. She wanted to go to New York someday and model. Sally told her a lot about it." Her eyes glistened. "I stood right here and talked to her. And now she's dead."

Bethanne hugged her. "I know how you feel."

"Boy, I could tell you tales," Sally said. "I remember . . ."

Bethanne stepped toward the door. According to Sally, modeling and New York were all that really mattered. She reminisced every chance she got. Bethanne used to come to the shop just to hear Sally talk about the big city and the glamorous life she'd led there. But after a while, the stories all started to sound the same.

"Sorry, but I've got to go," Bethanne said. "I'll call Dot and get everything settled." She waved and left the shop.

When Bethanne drove into her driveway, Boxer met her. He held his leash in his mouth. She looked at her watch. Three o'clock. She had time. And she had promised him. Reaching around, she swung the back door open, and Boxer jumped in the car.

Bethanne drove two blocks to a small neighborhood park. She pulled a worn tennis ball from the glove compartment, then hooked on Boxer's leash. They walked down a brick path to the center of the park where shade trees and benches surrounded a gurgling fountain. Around it, water pooled in a basin. In an area to the left stood climbing bars, swings, and a slide. Several small children played there, while mothers, some with babies in strollers, sat talking around the fountain.

Bethanne led Boxer to an open grassy area on the right. Taking off his leash, she tossed the ball. Like a shot, he rushed after it. They had played for about twenty minutes when she heard a child shout, "Birdman!"

Bethanne glanced toward the fountain. Birdman, in his long black overcoat and cap, was settling on one of the benches. Three of the children had joined him.

Birdman had lived in Valley since before Bethanne was born. He'd built a kind of shack with cardboard and plywood under the train bridge, where it crossed the river at Third Street. The police left him alone; he never bothered anyone.

23

Three years ago, when the river flooded and washed away his makeshift shelter, townspeople had built a wooden structure for him to live in.

He earned money by recycling for the city. His route covered a different area every day. He used some of the money he made for bird seed, which he fed to the birds at this park. Now, he held out a bag of seeds to the three children. Each took some of the food and scattered it on the bricks around the fountain.

Bethanne called Boxer, and they walked to the benches. Small birds flitted down from the trees and pecked around Birdman's feet. He held seeds in his hand, and a bird perched on his thumb and ate.

Bethanne stood behind a bench, recalling how she used to feed the birds with Birdman's seeds. Once, when she and Peri were about six, he let them climb up beside him. He'd put seeds in their hands. A sparrow had immediately flown down to perch on Peri's wrist. No bird came to Bethanne.

"Afternoon, missy." Birdman held out the bag to her.

She shook her head. She'd love to have a bird eat from her hand, but she was afraid none would come. That would be too embarrassing in front of all these people.

She led Boxer from the park and drove home. Her mom was in the kitchen, grating cabbage for coleslaw.

"How'd the interview go?" she asked Bethanne.

"I got the job."

"Great!"

"I'll need the car some mornings," Bethanne said. "I hope that's okay."

Her mom nodded. "We'll work it out. How was Kris Kirk?"

"She's nice, but . . ."

Peri did say not to say anything, Bethanne thought. Mom's different. Maybe she'll have some advice.

"I stopped at BoTeek to tell Peri," Bethanne said. "She told me something kind of weird." With her finger, Bethanne traced the tile line on the countertop. "I promised to keep it secret, so . . ."

Her mom set the grater down. "It won't go any further."

"Okay, then. I would like to know what you think."

"Really strange," her mom said after Bethanne had related the thefts. "That kind of stuff can mean someone is asking for help. Maybe she feels like something in her life is out of control."

"Probably has to do with her husband," Bethanne said. "He's kind of creepy."

Her mom was silent a moment. "I'd almost forgotten, but that night they came to the council meeting, they were pitching a financial plan for investing the city's money. After they left, one of the council members said the deal was just to the right of illegal."

"What's that mean?" Bethanne asked.

"The way he explained it, it meant we would be gambling with the city treasury. If the consulting firm wasn't trustworthy, it could end up with all the money. It's a good thing he spotted the danger, because we'd all been impressed by the ideas."

"Should I trust them?" Bethanne asked. "Do you think they'll pay me?"

Her mom picked up the grater. "If they don't, you can always quit."

Bethanne laughed. "And meanwhile, I can spend my mornings lying around their pool. After seeing it, I would have worked for a lot less than they offered." The phone rang. "That's probably Dot," she said, heading to answer it. "Is it okay if I go to a movie this evening?"

"As long as the three of you stay together," her mom said. "The streets aren't safe anymore."

"Hi, Dot," Bethanne said when she picked up the phone.

Dot giggled. "How'd you know it was me?"

"I've already talked to Peri and all my boyfriends," Bethanne said.

"Boyfriends?"

Bethanne pictured Dot's blue eyes growing very wide.

"Think about it, Dot," Bethanne said.

Dot giggled again. "I get it. All your boyfriends is the same as no boyfriends."

"You didn't have to put it quite *that* way," Bethanne said.

"Oh, Bethanne, you could have lots of boys. You just have to loosen up. They all think you're not interested in them."

Dot—and Peri—had told her this plenty of times. But "loosening up" was harder than it sounded. And Bethanne didn't want lots of boys. Just Mark Stabler. Even thinking about him made her face warm. She'd never told Peri and Dot about how she felt. If she had, somehow it would get back to him. Then he would ignore her, and she'd know for sure she'd never get him. Keeping it secret let her dream.

"I got a job," Bethanne said.

Dot gave a loud sigh. "Okay, change the subject. I was just trying to help."

Now Bethanne laughed. She pictured Dot, her lips pressed tightly together so her dimples showed. Blond curls, big eyes, she looked like a favorite doll Bethanne had had as a child. Dot was tiny, too, only five feet. She'd used her size to her advantage. This year she'd placed third in the all-state gymnastic meet.

"I'm working in Forest Glen," Bethanne said, "baby-sitting for the Kirks. Great money!"

"They live by my grandmother," Dot said. "Maybe I'll come visit you someday."

"I'll check if it's okay," Bethanne told her. "We can lounge around the pool."

"Did Peri tell you about going to see a movie tonight?" Dot asked. "My sister wants to go, too. The Football Four insist on escorting all of us. Because of that killer, you know. So Steve and Brad will pick up you and Peri, and David and Jeff will take me and Lissa. They said to tell you they'll be around about seven. They'll bring you home, too. But maybe we'll go over to the Viking first."

"Sounds good to me," Bethanne said.

After the movie, Bethanne and her friends headed out of the theater. Suddenly, she stopped. "I left my sweater on the seat," she said.

"I'll wait for you," Peri offered.

"No, go ahead. I'll catch up." Bethanne hurried back into the dimly lit theater. She found the sweater and jostled her way through the movie-goers still crowding the lobby. Outside, she breathed deeply of the cool night air. Peri, Dot,

Lissa, and the Football Four had disappeared into the Viking Café two blocks down. The blue-and-gold sign jutted out over the sidewalk, a beacon on the dark street. She left the bright light of the theater marquee and headed there.

The shops along the way were closed and dark. The only illumination came from widely spaced streetlamps. By the time she reached the first corner, she was alone. Was it like this for those girls the Rosekiller had gotten? A quiet empty street, dimly lit? Had he jumped out from a shop door? Or snuck up on them, caught them from behind?

Footsteps sounded in back of her. She walked faster. The steps speeded up. She grabbed her throat, hunched her shoulders.

She didn't want to die!

A hand tugged Bethanne's arm. She shrieked. The hand dropped.

She turned around, then gasped. Mark Stabler stood there. Her face burned like a hot coal. She could still hear her stupid scream. He must think she was a real geek.

"I didn't mean to scare you." He spoke fast. She was glad he was looking at the sidewalk instead of her red face.

"You didn't," she said, rubbing her arm. It tingled where he'd gripped it. Now she wished he hadn't let go.

"When I came out of the theater, I saw you by yourself," he said. "I thought you might be going home. I read about the Rosekiller, how he likes pretty girls."

Bethanne's heart thudded. Was he saying he thought she was pretty?

Face it, Bethanne, she thought, dishwater blond hair and greenish-bluish-grayish eyes don't make pretty.

"I'm just going to the Viking. I forgot this," she said, holding out her sweater. "Everyone got ahead of me."

Now he looked at her. When her eyes met his, she felt like she was drowning. He smiled, and her knees wobbled.

"That's where I'm headed," he told her.

She touched her lucky earring. This is my chance, she thought. Come on, Bethanne, loosen up, like Dot said, and say something he'll remember forever.

Just then, Peri's head poked from the Viking's entrance.

"Hi, Mark." Peri raised her hand. "Bethanne, I was starting to worry about you."

Bethanne walked faster. She felt partly relieved she didn't have to think of something to say to Mark. Partly disappointed this chance was gone. He hadn't said anything either. He'd probably be glad to be rid of her.

Inside the Viking, Bethanne joined her friends in the center of the room. They'd shoved two tables together. The Football Four sat along one side. Bethanne had known them since she was small. Alone, each seemed different. In a bunch, following Dot around, they were four bodies with one brain.

The girls sat across from them. Bethanne took a chair between Dot and Lissa. Peri offered Mark a seat, but he shook his head. Giving Bethanne a small wave that sent her pulse racing, he joined two other boys in a booth.

This café was the hangout for Valley's high school students. Murals on the walls showed athletes wearing blue-and-gold Valley High Viking uniforms.

A waitress in blue pants and gold shirt set double cheeseburgers before each of the Football

Four. She added milk shakes, french fries, and onion rings. Leaving, she returned with Cokes and fries for the girls.

"We ordered for you," Peri told Bethanne.

Bethanne brought her attention back to the group. She'd been watching the booth where Mark sat. He had dark hair, dark eyes, and a runner's body—tall and lean. He'd moved to Valley just last fall. They both ran track in the spring, and she'd seen every one of his races. He'd kept to himself pretty much, even at the post-meet pizza parties.

"I'm glad you walked with Mark," Peri said. "I shouldn't have left you."

"Yeah," Steve said. "You girls better be careful until that Rosekiller's caught." He took a big bite of his cheeseburger.

"The cops came to our place today," Brad said, "to talk to my mom. She makes silk flowers. They wanted to check on the orders."

"Did they find anything?" Dot asked him.

"They didn't say, but I looked. The Rotary ordered a lot of roses for their Valentine dance last spring."

"My parents went to that," Dot said.

"Mine, too," added Bethanne. "So did probably half the grown-ups in Valley."

"BoTeek's a big customer—" Brad went on.

"That's because Sally changes the color scheme every month," Peri said.

"And the hospital gives a rose to everyone who has a baby. Mom had other orders besides, for restaurants and offices."

"What color rose does this guy leave?" David asked.

"They wouldn't tell my mom," Brad said. "I'm guessing red."

Bethanne pictured the girl she'd seen in the paper, lying still, eyes open, a red rose on her, like spilled blood. Goose bumps rose on Bethanne's arms. What if that hadn't been Mark on the street?

"Did the cops say anything else?" Peri asked.

Brad shook his head. "My mom mentioned the killer seemed to like tall, pretty girls. They just said 'Yeah.' You and Lissa should be real careful."

Bethanne looked at Lissa. She and Dot had been adopted. Each had blond hair and blue eyes, but Lissa was taller than Peri. Beautiful, too. Though a year older, Lissa often joined Dot and Peri and Bethanne. Bethanne had always liked her. She was fun, with a good sense of humor. She clerked for the local department store and also worked there as a model.

"Hey, Brad, you're scaring my sister," Dot said.

Brad looked down at his empty plate. The other boys smirked.

"But that's okay," Dot went on. "I don't want anything to happen to her."

Brad gave a smug smile.

"Lissa's pretty tough," Peri said with a laugh. She turned to Lissa. "Tell them what you did to that weirdo at the fashion show today."

Lissa joined Peri's laughter. "You know how Peri and I work in those fashion shows at the hotel restaurant every Saturday morning?" Lissa said. "We're supposed to stroll past the tables in the outfits. Talk to customers, tell them about the clothes. Today, a man—about thirty, I guess—was there with his wife. Every time I passed their table, he had some comment, kind of flirting. Like he thought he was hot stuff. It happens a lot, doesn't it, Peri?"

"I'd like to punch some of them in the mouth," Peri said.

Bethanne nodded. Peri had told her lots of stories like this.

"Anyway," Lissa went on, "I came around once, and his wife wasn't there. I was modeling linen pants and a silk blouse. When I got close to his table, he put a hand on my leg. He said he liked the outfit, but he liked what was inside it better."

"That creep!" Dot said. "You should have given him a karate chop." She slashed the air with a flat hand. "Like we learned in those lessons."

"I wanted to, but I didn't dare. I'd lose my job. I just told him to let go. Instead, he started moving his hand up. I jumped away. But I made sure my hand hit his coffee cup. Hot coffee spilled in his lap." Laughter bubbled in her voice. "He screamed he was burning up, so I dumped a glass of ice water on him. His face got so red, I thought he was going to explode."

Now, everyone was laughing. Bethanne glanced toward Mark's booth. She caught his eye, and he grinned at her. Surprised, she gave a quick smile before she turned away. Had she imagined that? She glanced back. He was still looking at her. Her heart thumped, and warmth spread up her neck. She took a large drink of soda.

"The manager, Mr. Lee," Lissa was saying, "brought a towel for the guy. By that time, his wife was back. She looked at the tipped coffee cup and the empty water glass and winked at me. She knew. In a loud voice, she thanked me for saving

33

her husband from a bad burn. Then she dragged him out."

Peri held up her hands. "And the best part— Mr. Lee congratulated Lissa on her quick thinking."

Brad's next words cut everyone's laughter short. "What if that guy's the Rosekiller?"

"His wife told me they were in Valley on business," Lissa said.

"But he could have been here for the other killings, too," Dot said.

"My dad thinks the killer could be someone advertising for jobs in the paper," Bethanne said. "When you call, he gets your address, then he gets you."

"My mom thinks it might be a cop," Peri said. "Girls wouldn't be afraid of a cop coming up to them."

"What about Birdman?" Lissa said. "He knows everyone."

"And he's weird," Jeff added. "Never talking. Wearing that black coat."

"Get serious," Bethanne said. "Birdman would never hurt anyone. Look how gentle he is with birds."

"Maybe. But birds aren't people," Jeff said.

Peri frowned. "I hate this. Everyone I look at could be guilty."

"Like me?" Steve asked. "Or Jeff? Or David?"

"Hey, Steve!" Jeff and David said together.

"We wouldn't run from you," Bethanne said.

"Yeah," Peri said slowly. "Like Bethanne wasn't scared to walk here with Mark."

Everyone looked toward Mark's booth.

"Wait," Bethanne said. "Mark's not the Rosekiller."

"If he were, he would have killed you," Peri told her.

"But you went out to find Bethanne, Peri," Dot said. "Maybe he didn't have a chance."

"Mark was my lab partner once in biology," Peri said. "He's pretty quiet, but he's okay."

Bethanne again glanced at Mark's booth. Could someone that cute be a killer? No, she wouldn't believe that. He had known the Rosekiller liked pretty girls, but he hadn't mentioned height. And he wouldn't have killed her anyway. She wasn't the Rosekiller's type. But Peri was, and Lissa, too. Bethanne never ever wanted to see their pictures on the front page of the paper.

Bethanne gazed at Peri. She was folding a napkin into a paper rose. Prickles climbed up Bethanne's back.

That night after Bethanne got ready for bed, she stared out her bedroom window. What an incredible day it had been. First, a great job. Then the Kirks. Kimmie, so sweet. Kris, a thief. Ken, creepy. And Mark Stabler. He'd talked to her, smiled at her. She placed a hand on her arm. She still felt the warmth of his touch.

The fear she'd felt before she knew it was him returned. Whining, Boxer bumped her leg. She stroked his head as she gazed out into the darkness. Was the Rosekiller out there right now, stalking someone? And why, when she thought of him, did she picture Ken Kirk?

6

Sunday morning, Bethanne went with her parents to visit her grandmother. She lived in a retirement home outside Valley. This grandmother was Bethanne's dad's mother, and her name was Anne. Bethanne's other grandmother had been named Beth. Since Bethanne's parents couldn't decide whom to call her after, they'd combined both names.

Bethanne loved both grandmothers, but the name Bethanne was so ordinary. She always wished for something unusual, like Peri, short for Periwinkle, a flower, or Dot, short for Dorothy.

Bethanne and her mom and dad took her grandmother to breakfast. Afterward, her dad offered to take her for a drive up into the Cascade Mountains, but she complained of coming down with a cold. They stayed at her apartment in the home for a couple of hours before leaving.

Off and on all day, Bethanne's thoughts went to Mark Stabler. Saturday night, almost every time she'd looked at his booth, he'd been staring at their table. Maybe he had meant it when he said she was pretty. She should have asked Peri and Dot what they thought. But then Bethanne would have had to admit she liked him. She still wasn't ready for the teasing that would bring.

Monday morning, low clouds blanketed Valley, the kind of clouds that should burn off by noon. After eating a quick breakfast, Bethanne fed Boxer, hugged him good-bye, then rode her bike to Forest Glen. The damp air cooled her as she traveled. Its scent was lush with the aroma of evergreens and late spring flowers.

Before Bethanne could knock, Kimmie opened the door. She had on a long, fluffy pink robe and pink bunny slippers. She stood in the doorway, index finger in her mouth, staring at Bethanne.

Bethanne smiled at her. "Can I come in?"

Nodding, Kimmie stepped aside. Just then, Kris appeared in the entry.

"Hi, Bethanne," she said. "There's coffee made." She wore a tailored pale gray suit and mint green pumps. Bethanne wondered briefly if the green scarf holding back Kris's hair had been stolen from BoTeek.

Kimmie grabbed Bethanne's hand and led her to the kitchen. The coffee aroma was strong. Bethanne stopped short. Ken Kirk sat at the counter, a steaming mug before him. He studied her for a moment with his snake look. Prickles ran up her back. He took a long drink.

"Time for work." Standing, he kissed Kimmie, called good-bye to Kris, and left the kitchen.

Seconds later, Kris came in. "Kimmie, go get dressed," she said.

When Kimmie left, Kris poured two mugs of coffee. Bethanne wasn't really a coffee drinker, but it pleased her that Kris included her, the way she would another adult. To make the coffee easier to take, Bethanne added three teaspoons of sugar. When she tipped the cream pitcher, cream flowed out quickly. She stopped just before the coffee overflowed. She sat on one of the high stools. Kris joined her.

"Did you get a chance to talk to Ken?" Kris said. "I know you'll like him."

"He seems nice," Bethanne said. She wouldn't tell how creepy he made her feel.

Kris sipped her coffee. "I owe him everything." She swung her arm around. "All this."

"I thought you worked together," Bethanne said.

"I owe him that, too," Kris said. "It goes way back."

Bethanne looked at her brimming mug. If she lifted it, the coffee might spill over. If she didn't, Kris might ask why. Carefully, Bethanne raised the cup.

"Have you ever been to New York?" Kris asked.

Bethanne's head shake spilled some coffee. She set the mug down and grabbing a napkin, dabbed at the counter.

"I grew up in a real poor section of New York," Kris said, seeming not to notice the spill. "My dad disappeared when I was about Kimmie's age. All I remember about him is the smell of alcohol and his screaming at my mother. I've got three brothers—one is younger—and two sisters. My mom worked two jobs—my oldest sister took care of us—to keep the family together."

Kimmie came into the kitchen. She had on a blue and green fish-patterned bathing suit and a straw beach hat.

Kris laughed. "Kimmie, it's too cold to swim yet."

Kimmie looked outside. Without a word, she left

the room. While Kris was talking to Kimmie, Bethanne managed to get the mug to her lips. She sipped the coffee, enjoying the creamy flavor. She wondered briefly why Kris was telling her these things.

"I met Ken," Kris went on, "when I was sixteen."

My age, Bethanne thought. Like I met Mark.

"My mother cleaned house for Ken's mother," Kris continued. "He was working as a stockbroker in those days. My mom got sick at work one day, and Ken brought her home. It turned out to be cancer, but we didn't know that then. He helped her in. I remember being so embarrassed about our apartment. He didn't seem to notice the shabbiness. Even then, I thought he was the handsomest man in the world."

He must not have looked at her the way he looked at me, Bethanne thought.

"After that, he came to visit a lot," Kris went on. "He always brought something nice for us. Toys for my brother. Special food for Mom as she got sicker. Even my senior prom dress. At first, my mom argued about the gifts. He said he didn't have brothers and sisters, and he liked our family. When his mother died unexpectedly, he just kind of became one of us. He made it possible for me to go to college. He never said a word about being interested in me until I graduated. That day, he asked me to marry him. Of course, I'd loved him forever, but I never suspected he felt like that about me."

Bethanne sighed. Just like her with Mark. Was he loving her in silence? Yeah, sure, Bethanne, she thought. And you're Miss America.

Kimmie reappeared, dressed in a bright red snowsuit.

"Kimmie, it's summer," Kris said. "Snowsuits are for winter."

Kimmie's face crumpled. "Then I don't know what to wear."

Kris crouched and pulled her close for a hug. "Put on your blue shorts and your sweatshirt, like Bethanne."

Kimmie studied Bethanne. "Okay." Kimmie left.

Laughter in her eyes, Kris shook her head. "You sure you want her?"

Bethanne nodded. "My dog was to take the place of the little sister I begged for for years. She's great."

Kris's shrug turned her hands palm up. "Anyway, you can see why I'd do anything for Ken."

Again, Bethanne wondered why it was so important she know this.

Kris looked at her watch. "I've got to go to the office. I'll explain the computer tomorrow." She picked up a briefcase sitting beside the stool. "Meanwhile"—she grinned at Bethanne—"you two have fun at the mountains and seashore."

Bethanne laughed. "Sure. Maybe Wednesday I'll bring my snowsuit."

After Kris left, Bethanne and Kimmie played dolls and held a tea party inside. When the sun broke through the clouds, Kimmie took her outside to climb on the big wooden jungle gym. Then, they built an elaborate castle in the sandbox.

Kris arrived home at noon with a promise to Kimmie of McDonald's for lunch. Bethanne pedaled home. She and her mom sat at the umbrella table in the backyard, eating tuna sandwiches and drinking iced tea. The sun shone bright on the rows of peas, lettuce, and other vegetables in the garden. Boxer lay in the shade under the table. His head rested on Bethanne's foot.

Bethanne recounted Kris's story about her early life. "It was like she was trying to explain herself or something. Really weird," Bethanne said. "One thing for sure. She really loves Kimmie. Probably one of the reasons she's so grateful to Ken." She chewed a bite of sandwich slowly. "You know, Mom, the trouble is, when I'm around her, I just can't stop thinking about what Peri said. I almost wish she hadn't told me."

"It might help explain the shoplifting a little," her mom said. "Growing up very poor may have made her insecure, wanting more things. Maybe she suspects Peri knows about the stealing and is explaining why."

"But she doesn't know I know Peri," Bethanne said.

Her mom shrugged. "Well, maybe she realizes her husband comes on a little weird. She might be covering for him. Or she could just need to talk. He's a lot older than she. Kris may not have any friends her own age." She paused. "Speaking of talking, let's talk about your bedroom."

"Oh, Mom, it's not *that* bad," Bethanne said.

After lunch, Bethanne cleaned her room, then put her bathing suit on under her shorts and shirt. She was meeting Peri and Dot at Riverfront Park.

She needed suntan lotion, so first she biked west down B Street to the drugstore. The sign in front said TAYLOR DRUGS. Her great-grandfather, a pharmacist, had started it in the days when phar-

41

macists mixed prescription medicines by hand. Each following generation had continued the store and the profession.

Bethanne's dad had a scrapbook containing Taylor Drugs' early advertisements for over-the-counter remedies: medicines that promised to grow hair on men's heads, give energy, cure stomach ailments. She liked reading about the early medicines. One was a weight-reduction pill. Later, her dad told her, it was discovered the capsule had a tapeworm in it. Because of all the false claims and the dangers of the medicines, he said the government had created the Federal Drug Administration to police the drug companies.

Bethanne didn't know if she wanted to be a pharmacist. Of the sciences so far, math and physics were her favorites. Since taking a rocketry class in junior high, she'd been more interested in space flight than medicine. When she'd told her dad, he'd said she should follow her dream. "Just marry a pharmacist," he'd said with a laugh.

Inside the drugstore, the air was cooler. She waved to her dad. He stood at the counter in the back, working on a prescription. She dodged the displays of beach balls, thongs, and air mattresses to get to the side wall. It held rows of various suntan lotions. Selecting one, she took it to her dad to pay for it. He smiled at her.

"Off to Riverfront," she said.

"How'd your morning go?"

"Kimmie's great. Her parents are a little strange."

"At your age, all parents are, aren't they?" he asked.

"These more than usual," she told him, "but I don't have to take care of them."

"Good thought." He put the lotion in a bag. "Stay on the main streets."

"Daddy, it's daylight."

"Bethanne, we don't know anything about this Rosekiller. He might strike whenever the opportunity presents itself. And if he sees you alone on an empty road—"

"Okay, okay, I'll be careful."

He handed her the bag. "And use lots of this. Sunburn is dangerous."

Bethanne grabbed the sack. "This world is getting too complicated. I probably should just stay in bed."

She left and headed for the park. The sun beat down. She passed the Tollefson Building, enjoying the brief shade it gave her. Was Ken Kirk in there watching her ride past? She pedaled faster.

At the park, Bethanne stood gazing out over the beach running along the river's edge. Sunbathers and their towels hid most of the sand. Loud music from several radio stations clashed in the air. It was heady with the aroma of suntan lotions. The thought of the Rosekiller came suddenly. He could be one of those glistening bodies. Despite the heat of the day, a chill ran through her.

Beyond the beach, a dock extended into the slow-flowing river. Small children dug in the sand along its edge. Farther out, sunlight sparkled on the dark water. It was busy with swimmers and people floating on air mattresses and in inner tubes. Bethanne locked her bike and went to find her friends.

"Hi, Bethanne," voices called as she wove her way around beach towels.

Finally, she saw Dot and Peri stretched out on the sand near the lifeguard tower.

"You guys are getting really tan," Bethanne said when she reached them.

Dot rolled over. "Bethanne," she squealed. "Have we got something to tell you!"

Bethanne dropped down on the hot sand beside Dot. "What?" She pulled her T-shirt over her head.

Sitting up, Dot put her sunglasses on. "Mark Stabler asked Peri out."

Bethanne's stomach tied into a knot. She jumped up quickly, before Dot could see the tears, and busied herself taking off her shorts.

Rolling over, Peri struck Dot on the arm. "He didn't ask me out, you dummy. He knows John's my boyfriend. He said he wanted to meet me to talk about something."

"Yeah," Dot said, "but John's gone for the summer. Now's Mark's chance." She giggled.

Bethanne spread her towel and lay on her stomach. She couldn't look at her friends. How could she ever have thought Mark could be interested in her when Peri was around?

"I'll put lotion on you," Dot said. She rubbed the creamy liquid on Bethanne's back. The coconut aroma wafted around them. Bethanne would never like that smell again.

"Where are you meeting him?" she asked. She tried to keep her voice light. She didn't want them to know how she hurt inside.

"At the Viking," Peri said. "Five o'clock, when he gets off work."

The Viking! After Saturday night, Bethanne had pretended the café was a special place for her and Mark. Hadn't their eyes met across the room? Hadn't he smiled at her for the first time? But he'd really been looking at Peri. Bethanne had just been in the way. She was a fool. The restaurant might as well burn to ashes for all it meant.

Dot started on Bethanne's legs. Bethanne felt sand gritting under Dot's fingertips.

"Bethanne," Peri said, "I think Mark's really interested in you."

Bethanne's heart thumped. What did Peri mean by that?

Dot asked Bethanne's next question. "Then why would he ask you out, Peri?"

"I got to know him a little in biology," Peri said. "He's kind of shy. I think he wants to know if Bethanne will go out with him. So he doesn't ask her and get turned down, I mean."

"Would you go out with him?" Dot asked Bethanne.

Bethanne rolled over and sat up. She didn't want to commit herself. She'd feel like a fool if Peri was wrong about the reason.

"I guess so," Bethanne told them, "if I wasn't busy."

Peri laughed her throaty laugh. "Come on, Bethanne. I saw how you looked at him outside the Viking the other night. And how you two smiled at each other inside."

"Really?" Dot said. "How come I never know what's going on?"

"Because it didn't happen," Bethanne snapped. "I don't want to talk about it anymore."

She flopped back onto her stomach and switched on her radio. As music blared out, she closed her eyes. Was Peri right about how Mark had looked at her? Was there a chance? Should she hope? She touched her lucky earring. That was all she could do.

Around three o'clock, two of the Football Four showed up at the park. They organized a volleyball game. Bethanne tried to join in, but she couldn't concentrate on the game. After getting conked in the head twice by the ball, she went back to her towel.

Before Peri left to meet Mark, she hugged Bethanne.

"I'll call you as soon as I get home," Peri promised.

Bethanne watched her go. It would take a lot of courage to answer the phone.

Bethanne's family ate dinner outside that evening. Shadows lay across the patio and garden. The cooling air smelled of her dad's barbecued chicken. Boxer sat beside Bethanne's chair, ready to catch the bits she always dropped him. Bethanne had just buttered an ear of corn when the phone rang. The rule was "No calls at dinner." She fought to keep from jumping up and answering it. The answering machine clicked on.

"Bethanne," Peri said. "Call me."

That's all? Bethanne thought. Couldn't she have given me some clue? By not saying anything, was Peri saying she was wrong. Did Mark really want Peri?

Bethanne's stomach tightened. She had to know, face the truth.

She set the corn down. "I'm not hungry. May I be excused?"

Her mother looked at Bethanne's full plate. "You haven't eaten anything."

"Too much sun, I guess," Bethanne told her.

Her mom frowned, then felt Bethanne's forehead. "Maybe you better go to bed."

"I'll be okay. I'll just call Peri and relax."

"Sounds like that phone call is more important than my barbecued chicken," her dad said, laughing.

"Oh, Daddy . . ."

"Bethanne," her mom said, "eat your dinner."

Bethanne set the last dirty dish in the dishwasher and headed for the phone. Her parents still sat outside, drinking coffee. Bethanne picked up the receiver. She stared at it. Did she really want to know? She set it down.

The phone rang. She jumped.

"What did Peri say?" Dot asked when Bethanne answered.

"I was just going to call her," Bethanne said.

"Call me as soon as you know," Dot said and hung up.

Bethanne sighed. Now, she had no choice. Dot would hound her until she called.

Peri answered on the first ring.

"Tell me the worst," Bethanne said. She wanted this over.

"Has he called you?" Peri asked.

"No."

"Well, he's going to. He thinks you're really pretty."

Pretty? He was talking to Peri, looking at her, and he said I was pretty?

"He's been interested in you since he saw you on track," Peri went on. "He likes the way you practiced so hard."

Bethanne caught her breath. She hadn't known he was watching her. What about the meet when she tripped at the end of the two hundred meters? She'd felt like such a fool, sprawled on the track.

"He said," Peri went on, "when he saw you walking alone the other night, he got scared thinking about what could happen to you. With the Rosekiller, you know. That's when he realized how he felt."

Now Bethanne was warm all over. "Tell me again," she said.

"What?"

"About him calling me."

Peri laughed. "He's going to, so let's get off the phone."

"But what will I say?"

"Bethanne, I can't do everything for you. Talk about track or the movie or summer vacation. Definitely agree to go out with him. I don't want him to think I was just fooling around."

"Of course, I will." Bethanne made quick notes on a scrap of paper by the phone. "But call Dot and tell her. I don't want to tie up the line."

Bethanne set the receiver down. She looked at her notes.

Track.

"Did you run track before you moved here,

Mark?" Dumb question. He was too good to have just started.

Movie.

"Did you like the movie last night?" Dumber. Everyone liked it. So if he said no, what could she say?

"How are you enjoying summer vacation?" Dumbest! The same question her parents' friends asked her.

She slapped the paper down. What she wanted to ask him was if he ever daydreamed about doing something really great for the world. Or wondered what dying was like. Or worried about endangered species, like whales or those cute little spotted owls.

She lay her head on the kitchen table.

"Don't call," she whispered.

The phone rang.

Bethanne stared at the phone. It rang again. She picked up the receiver. "Hello."

"Hello. Can I speak to Bethanne?"

Her heart dropped to her stomach. "This is Bethanne."

"Hi. This is Mark Stabler. Remember, we walked to the Viking together from the movie theater?"

As if she'd ever forget.

"I was wondering," he said, "well, I was wondering if you'd like to go on a picnic Friday evening."

Picnic? But then they'd have so much time to talk.

"The forecast says the weather will be good all week," he said.

She took a deep breath. Wasn't this what she'd dreamed about, Mark calling her? And she had promised Peri.

"Friday's fine," Bethanne told him.

"Great," he said. "How about I pick you up at five-thirty? We can get some fried chicken or something and go to the park." He paused. "Wish I could talk more, but I have to go out to dinner with my dad now."

Oh, no! Now that he was on the line, Bethanne didn't want him to hang up. In the background, she heard his name called.

"See you Friday," he said.

Her mom came inside as Bethanne hung up.

"I'm going on a picnic Friday with Mark Stabler, a boy at school," Bethanne told her. She couldn't stop her grin.

"Best cure for too much sun I can think of," her mom said, laughing.

Tuesday morning, Bethanne returned to the Kirks' house. Again the morning was overcast, but the sun was already sending shafts of sunlight through the clouds. She spent the ride imagining the picnic with Mark. Would he kiss her good night? She felt really dumb—sixteen and she really didn't know how to kiss. A couple of guys had kissed her, but she hadn't kissed them back. She'd kiss Mark back for sure. But what if she did it all wrong?

Ken drove his shiny black car out as she approached the driveway. A sudden feeling of dread sent a shudder through her so strongly the bike wobbled. She grasped the handlebars tight and pedaled hard to keep her balance. He showed his teeth as he passed. She didn't smile back.

Inside, Kimmie, wearing yellow shorts and shirt, sat at the counter eating a waffle. Kris took that time to show Bethanne how to work the computer. After Kris and Kimmie left for preschool, Bethanne spent the morning typing titles into the computer. Before she left, she copied them onto a floppy disk. She left it in the kitchen for Kris to store at her office.

Wednesday dawned bright and sunny. Bethanne

52

and Kimmie spent the morning in the pool. By the time Bethanne left. Kimmie had smiled at her and laughed out loud several times.

Thursday morning, Kimmie hugged Bethanne before leaving.

"I wish I could stay home with you," Kimmie said.

"Me, too," Bethanne told her, "but I have to do work for your mom. I'll see you tomorrow."

"Can we play ball in the pool again, and you chase me?"

"Sure."

As Kimmie headed out for the car, Kris said, "I've got a breakfast meeting with a client. After that, I'll be coming home to work. Ken's holding an investment seminar in the office. It'll be pretty hectic there. I'll ring the bell when I get here so you won't be frightened."

All morning, Bethanne typed titles into the computer. She heard Kris come home but didn't go to meet her. The phone rang three separate times, each time with only one ring. Kris was picking it up.

After filling two pages with titles, Bethanne printed them out. Next week, for a change, she'd go to the library with the lists and start cataloguing the books. She looked around. Tons more books to do. Boring, boring. But she was making a lot of money. She wouldn't complain too loud.

The phone rang. It rang again, and again. Kris must be in the bathroom or something. Bethanne answered, but before she could say hello, Kris did.

As Bethanne started to set the receiver down, she heard Ken's deep voice. "Got your message, Kris. What did Mrs. Talbot want this time?"

Talbot. That was Dot's last name. Did he mean

Dot's mother? Grandmother? Bethanne put the receiver to her ear.

"She asked what was going on with her telephone stock," Kris said. "I thought you took care of her last month."

"I spent a lot of time with the old bird," he said. "I was sure I'd calmed her down. What'd she say?"

"Somehow she's gotten a copy of her holdings. It shows all the sales."

"What did you tell her?" Ken asked.

"I explained we'd moved the money into more lucrative stocks. She got real upset. Started ranting about how you two had talked about this before. Claimed you promised to tell her before you made changes. She demanded I tell her about the new stocks. I said you hadn't had a chance to fill me in, but I was sure she'd like your choices." Her voice took on a pleading tone. "I did my best. She insists on coming to the office tomorrow morning to go over her portfolio. She's going to find out we—"

"Not tomorrow," he said, interrupting her. "I've got a Rotary breakfast and after that a new client I can't miss. I'll call her. Smooth her feathers. You calm down, too."

"What if she tells someone?"

"Everything's under control. Remember, we have our plan."

"But, Ken"—Kris's voice held tears—"I don't know if I can go through with it. Now that I know—"

"Kris," he interrupted again, "you've always trusted me. Don't stop now. We've worked too hard. Now, take a deep breath and relax. How about a big smile for your favorite husband?"

"Okay, honey." Her voice was shaky.

"I'll see you later," he said.

Bethanne hung up after she heard Kris's receiver click. It sounded like Ken had a plan to increase Dot's grandmother's investments. What did Kris know that kept her from wanting to go through with it?

The Talbot family was one of the wealthier old Valley families. Dot's grandfather had died a couple years before. When Bethanne's grandfather died, her father had taken over his mother's finances. Bethanne's mom had explained women in Grandmother Anne's generation weren't taught how to handle money. Maybe Mrs. Talbot didn't understand investments either.

What was Kris afraid Mrs. Talbot would find out? Bethanne knew something about stocks. Anyone could buy stock in a company at any time. The price went up or down depending on how many people wanted the stock. If Ken bought stock and then the price went down, Mrs. Talbot had lost money.

At noon, Bethanne found Kris and said goodbye.

At home over lunch outdoors, Bethanne told her mom what she'd overheard.

"Sounds like they've made free with the money," her mom said, pouring salad dressing on her lettuce salad. "But investing is the Kirks' business. Mrs. Talbot hired them to do it for her. If they buy good stocks, things will work out."

"At first, I thought maybe they stole her money." Bethanne dropped a crouton for Boxer. He crunched it.

"It sounds like Mrs. Talbot thinks that, too,"

her mom said. "That's probably what Kris is afraid she'll tell someone. A rumor like that can destroy a business."

"I think I'll call Dot and see if she knows anything."

"Bethanne, don't you say a word about what you heard. Eavesdropping is bad enough."

"If anything's happened, I won't have to." Bethanne laughed. "You know Dot. To her *secret* is just a word in the dictionary."

After lunch, she called Dot. She worked part-time at her father's insurance business.

"Hi, Bethanne," Dot said when she came on the line. "When's the big date?"

"Tomorrow—a picnic," Bethanne said. "I'm trying not to think about it. I get too tense."

"Just be your own sweet self." Dot's voice took on a southern accent. "That's what my mom always says. Is that sexist?"

"Only if you tell the boy to just be his own macho self."

Dot was quiet for a moment. "I get it. The same for both, right?"

"Sort of," Bethanne replied, "but I don't want him to be like me. Then, I might as well date you."

Dot giggled. "Oh, Bethanne." From behind her came a cheer. "My dad's celebrating. He just sold a million-dollar life insurance policy. And guess who bought it?"

"A million dollars! You mean like if you die, someone gets a million dollars? I hope it's my long-lost uncle."

"You've never talked about him," Dot said.

"I was just kidding," Bethanne told her. "Who bought it?"

"That guy you're baby-sitting for. Ken Kirk."

9

"Ken bought a million-dollar policy?" Bethanne said.

"Shhh," Dot said, her voice dropping. "It's really a secret. It's for his wife. He doesn't want to leave her and their little girl without anything."

"That's great," Bethanne said. "He's a lot older than Kris."

Maybe he wasn't so bad. Maybe she shouldn't judge him by two meetings. But even those thoughts didn't erase the shiver his name brought.

"Great for my dad, too," Dot said. "He makes money on it."

"But Ken's a financial advisor. My dad said they sell insurance," Bethanne said. "Why didn't he sell himself some?"

"Dad asked that, too. Mr. Kirk said it might be a conflict of interest if he bought his own policy. I don't exactly understand what that meant. Dad said it didn't make much sense anyway, but he'd take the business." She giggled. "I've got to go. Dad's taking us out to lunch to celebrate."

Bethanne remembered the reason for her call. "How's your grandmother?"

"Grandma?" Dot said, her voice puzzled. "Fine . . . well, kind of strange. Tomorrow's the anniversary of the day my grandpa died. We have to go there for dinner. I remember last year. She got weird and held on to us and talked about how lucky she was to have us. Lissa gets out of the whole thing because she has to work, so I'll get it double." She gave a big sigh, then said, "Got to go, Bethanne. I'll call you later."

That probably explained Mrs. Talbot's problem, Bethanne thought as she hung up. She just needed extra attention right then.

She went upstairs to change. She was meeting Peri at Riverfront.

Friday, Bethanne woke with a feeling of excitement. Then she remembered. This was the day she was going out with Mark. She gazed out at the sun-bright morning. He'd been right about the weather.

While she got ready for work, her excitement turned to worry. All her concerns since he'd asked her out came flooding back. She didn't know what to wear. She didn't know what they would talk about. Maybe he really was interested in Peri. Maybe he was using Bethanne to learn more about her. Bethanne almost wished it would rain.

When she left, Boxer followed her into the garage. He barked as she started to roll her bike out. She reached for a dog biscuit, then stopped. She'd spent very little time with him lately. His whine added to her guilt. Boxer shouldn't feel sad on this special day. She could take him. Having him and Kimmie around would help keep her mind off Mark and the date.

She hurried back in. After getting permission to use the car, she called Kris.

"Sure, bring him," Kris said when Bethanne asked. "I won't tell Kimmie. She'll love the surprise."

In the garage, when Bethanne showed Boxer his leash, his mouth opened in a wide grin. His tail wagged his body.

"Okay, fella," she said, opening the car door. "Let's go."

At the Kirks', Kimmie met Bethanne at the door.

"I brought you a surprise," Bethanne told her.

Kimmie's face lit up. Taking her hand, Bethanne led her to the car, then lifted her so she could see in the window. Boxer pressed his nose against the open slit at the top.

"That's Boxer," Bethanne told her.

"Can I touch him?" Kimmie asked. "Can we go to the park?"

Bethanne set her down. "I'll ask your mom."

Kris agreed to the trip. After she left, Bethanne brought Boxer in the house. He lay down by the fireplace. Shaking with excitement, Kimmie squatted by him and patted his head. Boxer stretched out, his tail moving slowly back and forth.

"He likes you," Bethanne told Kimmie and received a broad smile from her in answer.

Bethanne scrambled her an egg. Kimmie insisted Boxer be given one, too. Breakfast finished, they all went out to the car. Just then, a red pickup pulled up behind it. Bethanne noticed piles of newspapers sitting outside the garage.

"It's Birdman, Bethanne," Kimmie said.

"I know," Bethanne told her. "He comes to my house, too."

Birdman got out of the truck. Boxer rushed to him. He patted the dog's neck, then touched his own forehead. "Morning, missy, little missy," he said.

"We're going to the park," Kimmie told him.

Grinning, he reached into the deep pocket of his coat. He pulled out a small bag of bird seed and handed it to Kimmie.

She looked up at Bethanne, eyes questioning.

"It's bird seed. To feed the birds at the park." Bethanne took the bag and put it in her shorts' pocket.

"Thank you, Birdman," Kimmie said.

He moved to the newspapers. Watching him, Bethanne remembered Lissa's words about Birdman being the Rosekiller.

Not possible, Bethanne thought. He's too nice.

She opened the car door, and Boxer and Kimmie climbed in the backseat. Boxer curled on his blanket. Bethanne buckled Kimmie in the child car seat Kris had left.

Birdman had loaded up the newspapers, and he backed out before Bethanne. He turned in the next drive. At that moment, Ken's car drove toward them. He passed with a wave.

Must have forgotten something, Bethanne thought. Good thing we're leaving.

She continued to her neighborhood park.

As they walked to the fountain, sunlight warmed Bethanne's cheeks. She breathed deeply of the fresh morning air. A large golden butterfly flitted around the pansies at the base of the fountain. She and Kimmie were the only visitors there.

Kimmie asked to feed the birds. Bethanne

opened the bag, and Kimmie dumped the seeds in a pile on the ground. Sparrows fluttered to the heap. They flapped their wings, chirping sharply in an argument over the food.

"They should share," Kimmie said.

Bethanne flung seeds in the air. "Let's spread it out."

Kimmie joined her. Then, as though they, too, had been tossed by handfuls, more and more birds flew down.

Boxer's bark flurried the sparrows. Bethanne led him and Kimmie to the grassy area. Kimmie's wild throws of the tennis ball had him scurrying all over the grassy field. When she tired of tossing the ball, she joined Boxer in chasing it. His yips, her excited cries joined the birds' incessant chirping.

When the two slowed down, they all walked back to the fountain. Tinny ice cream truck music filled the air. Bethanne bought three ice cream bars. Taking tiny bites from hers, Kimmie watched Boxer gulp his down. His long tongue licked the ice cream from his muzzle.

"He's messy," she said.

"That's good manners for dogs," Bethanne told her.

Kimmie rubbed some ice cream on her upper lip, then licked it off. She giggled. "Good manners for me, too."

Bethanne laughed with her. Kimmie was the little sister Bethanne had always wanted.

At noon, when Bethanne took Kimmie home, Kris gave Bethanne her first paycheck. She folded it and tucked it into her pocket. Her first step toward track camp.

"You have to face tonight now," Bethanne said to herself as she drove away. What to wear, what to say. She headed for BoTeek.

There she found Peri at the cash register, eating a sandwich.

"Big day!" Peri said with a grin.

"Don't say that," Bethanne said. "I'm already nervous enough."

"So what are you wearing?" Peri asked.

"That's why—"

At that moment, a thud came from the back room.

"What's going on?" Bethanne asked.

Peri sighed. "It's the reason I'm eating out here. Sally's pouting. We got the July issue of that fashion magazine she modeled for. One of the models is a woman she knew, her age." Peri voice dropped to a whisper. "You know how she always whines about being shut out of the job because she was too old. I think she was just too hard to work with."

"She is kind of annoying," Bethanne said, "the way she goes on about being a model. Like our lives aren't worth anything."

"This happened with last month's magazine, too," Peri added. "And last week, the hotel told her they didn't need her to model anymore in the Saturday show. She spends the whole show sneering about how amateur it is. Mr. Lee probably got tired of listening."

"You never told me about this before," Bethanne said.

"It's no big deal. The pay's good, and I love the clothes and the modeling. Now, back to the important subject. What are you going to wear?"

10

The doorbell rang at five-thirty. From the kitchen came answering barks.

"It's okay, Boxer," Bethanne called, hurrying to the entry. She touched her lucky earring, then opened the door.

"Hi, Bethanne," Mark said, smiling at her. He looked great in a white tank top that showed off his tan shoulders.

She wore her cream-colored walking shorts and Peri's cherry-red silk shirt. His look told her it had been worth the hour's work to get her hair to tumble over her shoulders just right.

"Come on in," she said. "I have a couple things we can take for the picnic."

"I got hot dogs instead of chicken," he said, following her to the kitchen. "I brought our little hibachi to use to barbecue."

Her mother stood at the counter, frosting a cake.

"This is Mark Stabler," Bethanne told her.

She held out a hand, then laughed. Chocolate frosting covered her fingers. "Don't shake it," she warned him. "Nice to meet you, Mark. Are you related to the new vet, Dr. Stabler?"

"He's my dad," Mark said.

"You tell him we're sure glad to have a small animal vet here. Used to have to take Boxer to north Seattle for his shots."

As if on cue, Boxer crawled out from under the table. He sat beside Mark and whined. Mark rubbed behind Boxer's ears. "Hi, fella."

"He's my dog," Bethanne told Mark. "But right now, you're his best friend."

"Bethanne tells me you're a pretty good runner," her mom said.

Mark's ears reddened. He squatted quickly and scratched Boxer's back. "I do okay," he mumbled.

Oh, Mom, Bethanne thought. Now he knows I talked about him.

To hide her discomfort, she turned and from the refrigerator took a covered bowl of potato salad. She placed it and a bag of chips in a small basket.

"All ready," she told him.

Carrying the basket, Bethanne led Mark to the front door. Boxer followed. As she stepped out, he whined and barked.

Mark laughed. "Looks like he wants to go, too."

"He doesn't have to," Bethanne said quickly.

Boxer barked again.

"We can take him," Mark said. "Does he like to play Frisbee? I brought one."

Now Bethanne laughed. "He thinks he's the best Frisbee player in the world. He'll do just about anything to catch it."

"My dad keeps leashes in the car," Mark said, holding the door wide open.

Boxer cocked his head.

"Okay, boy, you can come," Mark told him.

Boxer bounded out.

Bethanne grabbed her jacket. "You just set

yourself up as Boxer's all-time favorite person," she told Mark.

"That's a start," he said, smiling at her.

Does that mean he wants to be mine, too? She touched her lucky earring. As if he isn't already.

They climbed in the car, Boxer in back, his head out the window.

Mark snapped the stereo on. "This station okay?" he asked.

"My favorite," she told him.

They rode without talking, heading for the park. Sunlight shone through the open window, warming Bethanne's shoulder. The air smelled of freshly cut grass.

I have to say something, she thought, or he'll think I'm a real dork. What did Peri say to talk about?

She couldn't remember. Being this close to Mark made everything fly out of her mind. Just then, Boxer put his paws on the back of the seat. That gave her an idea.

"Are you going to be a vet like your dad?" she asked.

"He wants me to. But I don't know. I'm working at his clinic this summer to get a feel for the job."

"I know what you mean," Bethanne said. "My family's had a pharmacist in it since Valley started. I know Dad would like me to be one, too." She rested her arm on the window ledge. The breeze rippled her sleeve. Talking to him wasn't as hard as she'd thought it would be.

"Do you ever feel like you should know by now?" she asked. "I mean, like Peri already plans to be a model, and Dot wants to be a gymnastic coach. Even the Football Four have decided to be professional football players." She paused. "Sometimes I feel so ordinary because I don't have any great plans." Her admission surprised her. She'd never even told that to Peri or Dot.

"You're not ordinary," he said.

His words swelled in her chest. Not knowing how to respond, she peeked at him. His cheeks were flushed.

He really is kind of shy, Bethanne realized. Like me. That thought made her feel more comfortable.

"I've thought about the future," he said, his face serious now. "What I think is that it might be better to take time to look around. Then you know about a lot of different kinds of jobs. If you ever get tired of one, you have other choices."

Bethanne leaned back in the seat. She liked rocket science kinds of things, but she also liked history a lot. This year she was taking archaeology. She was real excited about that. Mark's idea meant she could be a scientist, then a history teacher, then an archaeologist. Maybe even fit in pharmacy. That made the future sound like fun. And not ordinary.

"I like that idea," she told him.

Another smile set her heart pounding.

They had reached the park. At the end, beyond the bathing beach, stretched a wide grassy area. Several families had already set up picnics on the tables scattered throughout the space. Mark parked the car, then pulled a leash from the glove compartment. While she attached it to Boxer's collar, Mark took a large box out of the trunk. He added Bethanne's bowl of salad and the chips, and she and Boxer followed him to a table near the water.

After setting up the hibachi and lighting the coals, Mark pulled out the Frisbee. Boxer's ears perked up and he barked, then jumped for the toy.

Unleashing him, Bethanne said, "Throw it."

Mark flung the Frisbee and Boxer took off. He leaped high, twisting back to catch it.

"Wow," Mark said. "He should be on TV."

"Told you," Bethanne said.

They played Frisbee, laughing at Boxer's gyrations, until the coals were hot. Mark barbecued six hot dogs, and with Boxer's help, all were eaten. To Bethanne's pleasure, conversation came easily, one topic leading to another. When they talked about track, Mark said he planned on going to track camp in August. That news sent Bethanne's heart racing. He seemed equally pleased to learn she was going.

After dinner, they toasted marshmallows. When they'd had their fill, they sat on a blanket in the dusk, watching the setting sun.

The day had cooled, and they both had put jackets on. Mark draped his arm around Bethanne's shoulder. He rested his head against hers.

"You smell good," he said.

"I do?" She hadn't worn any perfume.

"Like barbecue smoke and fresh air and sunshine," he said.

"My own perfume." She laughed. "I call it Picnic."

He was silent a moment, before he spoke again. "You know, I was a little worried about going out with you."

You were? she thought. You should have seen me before you came. Like a scared rabbit.

"I didn't know you'd be so easy to talk to," he went on.

I probably should admit it. "I felt the same way about you."

"I guess we were both surprised," he said.

His arm tightened around her. She leaned against him, loving the way it felt.

Boxer plopped his head on her lap. He looked up at her, his eyes pleading.

"Sorry, Boxer," Mark said. "We haven't been paying attention to you." He checked his watch. "We probably should get going. I don't want your parents to worry about you. With that killer loose, I mean."

Bethanne hadn't thought about the Rosekiller all afternoon. She didn't want to think about him now. She got slowly to her feet. Boxer bumped against her legs.

Darn you, Boxer, she thought. If you had stayed away, he might have kissed me.

By the time they packed up and climbed into the car, night had fallen. The air was still warm, and they opened the windows.

I'll ask him in for cake, she thought. He'll kiss me then.

He turned onto her street, slowing as he neared her house. Boxer, whose head hung out the back window, barked. Mark and Bethanne both jumped at the sound.

"Boxer, stop!" Bethanne said, but the dog kept on.

"Look!" Mark pointed at the tall fir in the

corner of Bethanne's yard. "Someone's standing there." He pulled up to the curb and slammed the brakes on.

Bethanne peered at the tree. "It's just the tree's shadow from your headlights," she said.

Boxer was still barking.

"No," Mark said. "Something moved." Opening the door, he jumped out. Boxer struggled into the front seat and followed. Racing to the tree, he sniffed around the base, then along the tall rhododendrons bordering the fence at the lot's edge.

Her parents came out of the house.

"What's Boxer barking at?" her mother called when she saw Mark.

"Someone was by the tree," Mark said.

By then, Bethanne was out of the car. She joined them walking across the wide front lawn. As they neared the fir, the dark closed in around her.

You're being silly, she told herself. There's nothing there. Mark just thought he saw something because of Boxer's barking.

Nevertheless, she scooted closer to her parents. Reaching the tree, Mark pushed aside the long branches. A spicy scent filled the air.

"See anything?" Bethanne's dad asked.

"Yeah," Mark said, "I do."

He bent to the grass. When he stood, he held a red silk rose.

11

"I don't understand why you're not doing something," Bethanne's dad said.

After the rose discovery, he had gone into the house and called the police. Dan Reid had come, bringing two officers. With flashlights, they searched the bushes on both sides of the fence. They found some broken branches in the neighbor's yard, but nothing to suggest for sure someone had hidden in the bushes there.

"Daddy," Bethanne said. She sat on the couch by Dan. "They looked all over out there. What else can they do?"

"Bring dogs or something," her dad said, pacing back and forth in front of the fireplace. "Track him down."

Dan patted Bethanne's hand. "We don't know for sure someone was there," he said.

"The rose!" Her father stopped pacing abruptly. "Someone left it. And what about Boxer? He barks when any person comes on our property. Mark saw someone, too."

Mark, Bethanne thought. He'd left after telling Dan what he'd seen. She knew he'd been embarrassed to be put on the spot with so little to report.

And Dan had asked him over and over what he'd noticed. Even took him out in the car to re-create the event.

Mark had continued to insist someone had been by the tree. He'd gone so far as to suggest Bethanne's dad be very watchful of her. She liked knowing Mark cared about her, and when he held up that rose, her heart *had* dived for her feet. But she didn't need to be looked after like a baby.

Her dad had agreed with Mark, and her mom sided with her dad. From now on, they'd monitor every move she made. The way her dad's anger was growing right then, pretty soon she'd be locked in a tower, like Rapunzel.

"The rose could have been left earlier," Dan said. "And the color's—" He stopped abruptly. "Well, anyway, Boxer and Mark might have been looking at the tree's shadow. A small breeze could make it seem like something moved. I know you're worried, Jack. So am I. We're following every lead we have, but there aren't many. This guy's pretty smooth." He stood and put on his chief's hat. "One of these days, he'll make a mistake."

Face red, her father stopped in front of Dan. "He's after my daughter. I don't want to wait for him to make a mistake. I want you to catch him. Right now." His fist slashed down, punctuating the last words.

Bethanne's mother moved beside him and linked her arm with his. "There are other girls living on this street. He could have been waiting for someone, anyone to come along. Not necessarily Bethanne. Dan's doing what he can. He cares about her, too."

His shoulders sagged. "I know. I'm sorry, Dan. It's just that . . ."

Dan waved a hand. "Don't apologize. In the last month, I've seen three young girls killed. It's hell."

His words brought Bethanne face-to-face with the terribleness of what was happening. What if she hadn't gone with Mark? What if she'd just stepped out to smell the night air? Or wish on a star. She did that sometimes. The Rosekiller would have put a rope around her throat and pulled it tight. She put her hand to her neck, and a shudder ran through her. This wasn't about whether she needed to be watched over or not. This was about her life.

She had a sudden thought. "How about the landscaper?" she asked her dad.

He snapped his fingers. "Right. Get that newspaper, Bethanne."

"Come on, Boxer," she said. Boxer wasn't much of a bodyguard, but he'd let her know if a stranger lurked in the garage.

She snapped on all the lights on the way to the garage. When she returned with the paper, her parents and Dan were by the phone in the kitchen. Her dad was explaining about the call to the landscaper.

"Bethanne left her name," her dad said. "No reason the guy couldn't have found her. This is a small town."

When she got the number from the paper, Dan dialed. He listened, then hung up.

"It's been disconnected," he said. "Tomorrow, I'll check on the number with the phone company."

"Sure," her dad said, his voice suddenly tired. "He got enough names. Now, he's acting on them."

After Dan left, Bethanne headed for bed. Her mother stopped her. "Are you okay, Bethanne?"

She nodded. "It's pretty scary. I'm not going to take any dumb chances. Maybe from now on, I should drive to work instead of bicycling. I know he always does things at night, but . . ."

Her mom hugged her, hard. "Seeing that rose was about the greatest shock I ever had. I get goose bumps just thinking about it." Stepping back, she rubbed her arms. "I'm glad you're going to be sensible about this. We'll work out the car arrangements."

"Thanks, Mom."

The phone rang. Her mom looked at her watch. "It's midnight. Who would be calling?"

Bethanne returned to the kitchen and picked up the receiver slowly. "Hello."

"Bethanne, have you seen my sister tonight?" Dot asked.

Bethanne collapsed into a chair. "No, Dot. But wait until you hear what happened—"

"Bethanne," Dot interrupted, "we just came home from my grandmother's. Lissa got off work two hours ago, but she's not here."

"She probably went to a friend's," Bethanne said.

"She knows how my parents are worried about the killer. If she did that, she would have called my grandmother's." Dot's voice was thick with tears. "I'm so afraid something has happened to her."

The Rosekiller got her. That's what Dot's thinking. As long as we don't say it, it won't have happened.

"Can I do anything?" Bethanne asked, trying to keep the fear out of her voice.

"Would you call Peri and ask? And the Football Four? My parents are out driving around, looking. I'm going to start calling her other friends."

"Sure, Dot. And don't worry. I'm sure she's somewhere safe."

Dot sniffed. "Thanks, Bethanne. I'll talk to you later."

Hanging up, Bethanne let the worry rise up. "Lissa's missing."

Her mother paled and clapped her hand to her mouth. "Oh, no."

"Dot wants me to call around, see if I can find her." Chest tight, Bethanne dialed Peri's number.

Her parents stayed with her while she phoned. No one she called had seen Lissa that evening. Bethanne tried to reach Dot to tell her, but got a busy signal.

"She's all by herself," Bethanne said, "and really upset. If the line is busy, it means she hasn't found Lissa. I think I should go over there."

"I'll drive you," her dad said.

"I'll go, too," her mom added.

At Dot's, Bethanne knocked on the front door. Dot peered out the door's small window. She let Bethanne and her parents in.

Dot's eyes were red; her cheeks, tear-streaked. "Did you find her?"

When Bethanne shook her head, the tears began again.

"My parents aren't back," Dot sobbed. "It's not that big a town. They could have driven around it twice already. And Lissa never stays out like this. Something terrible has happened, I know."

Fear swelling in her chest, Bethanne hugged Dot.

"Maybe she's been trying to call," Bethanne's mom said. "You've been on the phone."

"Do you think so?" Dot said, her face brightening a little.

The phone rang.

"That's her," Dot cried, hurrying from the entry.

They followed her to the kitchen.

"Hi, Dad, did you find her?" Dot was saying as they entered.

Her mouth dropped open. "No!" she screamed. "No, no, not Lissa." Bethanne rushed to her.

Bethanne's father grabbed the receiver from Dot. "Hi, Wes, it's Jack Taylor. We came over with Bethanne to check on Dot."

His hand gripped the phone until his knuckles shone white. Jaw clenched, he nodded once, then again. "We'll be there." He hung up.

"The Rosekiller attacked Lissa tonight," he told them.

I knew it, Bethanne thought, holding Dot tight. I knew it even though I didn't want to think it.

Her mother placed a hand on Bethanne's shoulder. Bethanne looked at her. This could have been you, her eyes said. Bethanne held Dot tighter.

"Is she . . . ?" Bethanne whispered.

Her dad shook his head. "She fought him off, but she's in a coma at the hospital. I told your dad we'd take you there, Dot."

Dot threw on a jacket, and they all drove up the hill north of town to River Ridge Hospital. When they entered, Dot's mother came running to them.

Her eyes were puffy from crying. Her face sagged with worry. She hugged Dot, then pulled her to the elevator.

When Bethanne and her parents didn't move, Dot's mom said, "Come with us."

"Please," Dot grasped Bethanne's hand. "Lissa would want you to be there. Me, too."

Upstairs, outside the hospital room, a policeman sat. Dot's mother spoke quietly to him, and he waved them all into the room.

Bethanne stared openmouthed at Lissa. Eyes closed, she lay still in the bed. Scrapes and bruises mottled her face. One cheek was purple. A white bandage wrapped her head, and a fiery red ring circled her neck. Beside her a metal stand held a bag of liquid, which dripped into a tube ending in her arm.

"Poor Lissa," Bethanne whispered. Her mother squeezed her shoulder.

Sobbing, Dot sat in a chair beside the bed. "Is she going to get better?" she asked as she stroked Lissa's hand.

"We hope so," her dad said, shaking Bethanne's father's hand. "They can't find any brain damage, thank goodness. It's just a matter of waiting for her to wake up."

"But she will, won't she?" Dot said, her voice hushed. "She won't stay like this forever."

Her mom shook her head. "All the doctor would say is that these things take time."

Dot leaned close to Lissa. "Wake up. You have to wake up."

"Keep talking to her," her dad said. "The doctor said that might help."

"Where did they find her, Daddy?" Dot asked.

"Three blocks from the store. The floor manager walked her out to her car after closing. That's the new policy because of the killer—" His voice broke, and he was silent for a moment, then continued. "No one knows why she stopped. There's nothing wrong with the car. The police think the killer somehow got her to open the door. Then he threw the rope over her and tried to drag her out. You know your sister." He patted Dot's shoulder. "She's never let anyone make her do what she doesn't want to. That spirit, and karate, saved her life. They think she hurt the killer. They found blood—not hers—on the pavement."

"Who found her?" Dot said.

"A man driving down the street," her dad said. "He saw her fighting with the killer. That's when the killer threw her down hard on the sidewalk. Fractured her skull. He took off. The driver thought he should take care of Lissa rather than chase the attacker."

"Did he leave a rose?" Bethanne's dad asked.

"No. Probably in too much of a hurry to take the time."

"Why is that policeman out there?" Dot asked.

"Lissa is the only person who can identify the Rosekiller," he said. "They don't want anything to happen to her."

"You mean the Rosekiller might come here to get her?" Dot cried. "I saw that once on TV. The murderer tricked the cop into leaving and got into the room." She stood. "I think I'll stay here tonight."

"I know Lissa would like your company," her mom told her. "The nurse can get you a cot."

"We better go," Bethanne told her parents. She

hugged Dot. "I'll call you tomorrow. Maybe she'll be awake by then."

At home, after Bethanne got ready for bed, she stood staring out her window into the black night. When the Rosekiller left Bethanne's yard, he must have gone to find another victim. Last Saturday at the Viking, Brad warned Lissa to be careful. What made her take a chance and open the car door? When Mark held up the rose, Bethanne had a sudden vision of Ken Kirk. Did Lissa know him? Through her grandmother, maybe? Had Lissa stopped to say hello? What about the man she'd spilled coffee on? No way she would've stopped for him. Maybe she'd pulled over for some other reason and had been attacked. Maybe, the landscaper . . . maybe . . . Bethanne pressed her hands to her temples to stop the whirling thoughts.

I hope Lissa hurt him. Really, really hurt him.

As she climbed into bed, Mark filled her vision. The image was replaced by Lissa's battered face. How could a day that started out so great end up being so bad?

12

Around ten-thirty the next morning, Bethanne drove to the hospital. This time, a policewoman sat outside the door to Lissa's room. She asked Bethanne for identification, and Bethanne showed her her driver's license. After checking a list, the officer waved Bethanne in.

Inside, Dot sat by the bed reading to her sister. Lissa looked as though she hadn't moved since Bethanne had seen her the night before.

"Hi, Bethanne," Dot said, looking up.

Bethanne gasped. Dot looked terrible. Circles under her puffy eyes were dark as bruises. Her hair was uncombed, and her clothes were wrinkled.

Like she slept in them, Bethanne thought. Her eyes went to a cot standing against one wall. Probably did.

"How's she doing?" Bethanne asked.

Tears filled Dot's eyes. "Nothing's changed. I keep squeezing her hand, but she never squeezes back."

Bethanne placed a hand on Dot's shoulder. "Give her time."

"I wish it were me lying there instead of her," Dot said.

Bethanne pulled her from the chair. "Call your

mom and have her pick you up. I'll stay and read to Lissa. You go home and get some sleep. If she woke up right now and saw you, she'd be scared back into her coma."

Dot ran her fingers through her hair. "I look pretty awful, huh?"

"Nothing a shower and nap won't cure. Now go."

Dot frowned. "You won't let that killer touch her?"

"He won't even get close."

Dot took her jacket from the back of the chair. "Thanks, Bethanne."

Bethanne sat down and opened the well-worn book. "Oh, *Winnie the Pooh,* my favorite."

"Lissa used to love that book better than anything," Dot said. "It's probably dumb, but I thought she might like it now. Think it's okay?"

"I think it's great. Now go. I'll see you later."

Dot left, and Bethanne started to read. She'd finished two stories when she heard voices outside. She stepped out. Steve and Brad stood by the policewoman.

"We came to see Dot," Steve said. "She"—he gestured to the policewoman—"won't let us in."

"She's guarding Lissa," Bethanne told him. "When she wakes up, she'll be able to identify the killer."

"Well, it's not me," Steve grumbled. "How's Lissa? Where's Dot?"

"Lissa's still in a coma," Bethanne said. "I sent Dot home. She needed to rest. She's really suffering."

"Can we do anything?" Brad asked.

Bethanne held up the book. "The doctor told

Dot's parents reading aloud and talking to her might help. And I know Dot would appreciate your support."

"No problem," Steve said. "Work out a schedule and let us know."

They left, and Bethanne returned to her reading. A short while later, Peri walked into the room. "Where's Dot?" she asked as she returned her license to her wallet.

"I sent her home," Bethanne said. "She was here all night, and I don't think she got any sleep."

Peri stopped and stared at Lissa. Her eyes went to the book Bethanne held. "Can she hear us?"

"I hope so," Bethanne said.

"I can't believe anyone would do this to her," Peri said. "I'd like to rip the guy apart."

"The cops think she hurt him," Bethanne said.

"Good," Peri said. "Is there anything I can do?"

"Call the Football Four and work out a schedule to come in and read to her. It might help bring her back."

"Sure," Peri agreed. "Anytime's good for me."

"What about BoTeek?" Bethanne asked Peri.

"Sally called this morning. Her sister in Seattle is sick, and Sally's going to stay with her. She's closing the shop for a week. When I told her about Lissa, she felt real bad."

Bethanne stayed at the hospital until three o'clock. Then, Peri took over. She brought a science fiction novel, since that was what Lissa usually read.

She and the boys had worked out reading times. They insisted the girls read only during the day.

Being out at night was too dangerous for them. As Lissa's other friends heard about the readings, they'd help, too.

When Bethanne reached home, her mom said, "Mark called you. His number is by the phone."

Bethanne's heart thumped with relief. She'd worried, after everything he'd gone through last night, he might not want to see her. She called him.

"Hi, Mark," she said when he answered. "It's Bethanne."

"How are you doing?" he asked.

She told him what happened to Lissa.

"That's terrible," he said. "He must have gone after her because he didn't get you."

"I almost feel guilty thinking that."

"He might have killed you," Mark said. "At least, she's alive."

"And can identify the killer," Bethanne said. "They're waiting for her to wake up and do that."

"I hope she does pretty soon," he said. "I've really been worried about you."

Bethanne smiled, pleased by his concern. "Thanks, Mark. After seeing what happened to Lissa, I'm not going to take any chances."

"I'd like to get together with you tonight," he said, "but I don't think you should go out of the house."

"Neither do my parents. Me, too, I guess," she said, "but—but we have a VCR. If you want to come over, we could rent a movie."

Please say yes. Please, please.

"Sounds great," he said. "About eight? I'll pick one up. Do you want funny or suspense?"

"Nothing scary," she told him. "I've had enough of that."

Monday morning, Bethanne delayed going to work until the last minute. She didn't want to run into Ken.

Clouds had moved in overnight. She drove her mom's car through the light rain to the Kirks', breathing a sigh of relief when she saw his car was gone.

Kris let Bethanne in, then left to finish dressing. Kimmie, in her robe, sat watching TV cartoons in the family room. She jumped up when she saw Bethanne.

"I'm going to the zoo in six days," Kimmie said. She held up the fingers of one hand.

Bethanne added another finger from Kimmie's other hand. "Six," Bethanne said.

"I'm going to see a nelephant," Kimmie said, "and a tiger and a lion. They're wild animals, Bethanne, not like Boxer."

"I know," Bethanne said. "They're big, too."

"Mama said they can't hurt me." Kimmie's face was serious. "They're in cages, and they can't get out."

Bethanne picked her up and carried her into the kitchen. "You know what else you'll see? Little monkeys. Like you." Bethanne tickled her and Kimmie giggled.

Bethanne set her on a stool at the counter. "How about breakfast?"

"What do monkeys eat?" Kimmie asked.

"Bananas."

"That's what this little monkey wants," Kimmie said.

"They like orange juice and toast and cereal, too," Bethanne told her.

"Okay."

As Bethanne began Kimmie's breakfast, Kris came into the kitchen.

"I'm a monkey." Kimmie waved the half a banana Bethanne had given her.

"You are." Kris laughed. She nuzzled Kimmie's neck. "And a very nice one, too."

"I told Bethanne about the zoo," Kimmie told her.

"Oh, yes, the zoo," Kris said without enthusiasm. She poured a cup of coffee. "I need to talk to you, Bethanne." She didn't look at her.

Oh, no! What did I do?

"I . . . well, Ken, um, he . . ." Kris looked at her watch. "I have to go. I'll talk to you later." Grabbing up the coffee cup, she left the room.

That's it, Bethanne thought. Ken wants her to fire me.

She spent the rest of the morning playing with Kimmie and worrying about losing the job. She loved taking care of Kimmie. For sure, she didn't want to work in the drugstore. Trouble was, by now, all the other summer jobs were probably taken.

When Kris came home at noon, she didn't say anything about the earlier conversation. Bethanne didn't bring it up either. She hugged Kimmie good-bye. Bethanne wouldn't think that it might be the last time she saw her. Outside, the rain had stopped. The sun, shining through broken clouds, had almost dried the streets.

At home, Bethanne's mom had placed a tray of strawberries on the kitchen counter. Beside that sat a large and small box holding peas from the garden.

"My first produce," she said. "I want to deliver it to the food bank."

Bethanne snapped open a pea pod and popped the peas in her mouth. "I'll go with you. Afterward, would you drop me at the hospital? My shift with Lissa is from two to four. I'll call Dad for a ride home."

Her mom touched the smaller box. "This is for Birdman. I had it ready Saturday, but he didn't show up. I thought I'd drop by his shack on the way. See if he's sick and needs help or something."

Bethanne ate a peanut butter sandwich. Then, she helped her mom carry the produce to the car. Boxer followed. He sat close to Bethanne while she put the food in the trunk. When she closed the lid, he gave a short bark.

"Okay, Boxer, you can come," she said.

His tail wagged.

They headed to Birdman's shack under the railroad bridge. On the way, Bethanne told her mom about Kris's strange behavior that morning. "Like she was embarrassed to talk to me or something. I can't think what I've done to get fired."

"I don't know how you can jump to that conclusion," her mom said. "From what you told me, all she did was mumble something about her husband."

"But she wouldn't even look at me."

"You said she seems to do what he wants. Maybe this is some idea of his she doesn't agree with. You told me he's strange."

Yeah, Bethanne thought. I wonder if he's got

scratches and stuff on him. Hey, that's it. He came home all scraped up, and Kris figured out why. She needs someone to talk to about it. Like Mom said before, I'm the only person she knows.

She pulled into Birdman's space under the bridge. An oil patch on the gravel marked where Birdman parked his pickup. Behind the space, tarps formed a shelter for piles of cans and newspapers.

"He's not home," Bethanne said.

"We can leave the peas," her mom told her. "Just set them inside the door."

Bethanne parked the car and climbed out. The bridge cast a shadow around her. The air felt cool, damp from the earlier rain. Even with a sweatshirt on, she shivered.

She took the peas from the trunk. Gravel crunched underfoot as she walked to the front door. Boxer trotted beside her, sniffing here and there. Bethanne knocked, just in case.

No sound came from inside. She turned the doorknob and pushed the door open slightly. Shoving against it, Boxer squeezed into the shack.

"Boxer," Bethanne called in a loud whisper, "get out of there." She peered in through the opening, then shouted, "Mom, Mom, come quick!"

Her mother came running. They both stood staring into Birdman's house.

Scattered on the neatly made bed in the corner were five red silk roses.

Bethanne and her mom stepped into Birdman's shack. Bethanne picked up one of the roses.

"It's like the one Mark found," she said, her voice hushed.

"We better go to the police station and see Dan," her mom told her.

"But, Mom, this doesn't mean Birdman's the killer. Maybe he found the roses in somebody's trash or something."

Her mom patted Bethanne's hand. "Dan would want to know that, too."

They left the shack, closing the door tight behind them, and climbed into the car. Boxer scrambled in behind.

Bethanne glanced back at the wooden structure as they drove away. In her mind, she saw Birdman seated on the park bench. A sparrow perched on his hand. Big hands, but gentle. Hot tears stung her eyes. "It can't be Birdman," she said.

"I know it's hard to imagine," her mom said. "I'm not ready to believe it either. But there's been a lot of postcombat trauma in Vietnam vets."

"Birdman is kind of strange," Bethanne said. "But he's always nice when he comes to our house. And look at how he takes care of the birds."

Her mom nodded. "Birdman's built a world here he can control. Lots of vets have coped that way. Trouble is, if something causes them to lose that control, their hold on reality can break down. If that happened to Birdman, who knows? Those girls might have seemed like the enemy to him."

Bethanne nodded. She'd seen movies where that kind of thing happened. But I won't believe it until I hear it from Birdman, she thought.

At the police station, they followed a policeman through a room that held two desks. Each was cluttered with a computer, telephone, stacks of folders, and coffee cups. On the walls, bulletin boards displayed wanted posters and work schedules. When Bethanne and her mom stepped into Dan Reid's office, he rose from behind his metal desk.

They told him what they'd seen at Birdman's.

"He didn't come for our recyclables Saturday," her mom said. "We stopped by because I thought he might be sick."

Dan picked up the phone and punched a button. "Get the license number for Birdman's pickup," he said into the receiver. "Then I want an all-points bulletin out for it. And a description of Birdman. I just want him for questioning, but care should be taken when he's approached. He may be dangerous." Dan stood. "I'll take a man over to check out his shack, see if we can figure out where he's gone."

"His father's a dentist in Seattle," Bethanne said. The thought brought the image of Birdman's smile. She blinked back tears.

I don't believe he did it. Even if he does have problems. Why would he want to kill me? Or Lissa? Or those other girls?

Dan put his arm around her shoulder. "I'm sorry,

honey. We have to pick him up. I need to know where the roses came from. It's for his protection, too. He may not be the killer. If the real one learns Birdman found the roses, Birdman's life could be in danger. In fact, for that reason, it's probably better you don't talk about this with anyone."

Just Peri, Bethanne thought. She won't tell. And she'll understand how I feel.

He hugged her. "We'll take good care of him, I promise."

At least he didn't think Birdman was the killer for sure. Bethanne forced a smile. "Thanks, Dan."

"Oh, by the way," he said as they opened the door, "tell Jack I checked on that landscaper. He is legitimate. Just looking for kids to help landscape that new office center up on the ridge."

Darn, Bethanne thought. I wish he'd been the Rosekiller. That would have been so easy.

After leaving, Bethanne and her mom dropped off the produce at the food bank. From there, they drove to the hospital. The policeman sitting at the door to Lissa's room waved Bethanne in.

After swearing Peri to secrecy, Bethanne told her about Birdman. Peri's eyes widened.

"Do *you* think he did it?" Peri asked.

Bethanne shook her head.

"But he could have," Peri said.

"I guess so."

"I don't want to believe it, either," Peri told her. "It makes me feel like I did when I found out there was no Santa Claus—like something hit me in the stomach."

"Me, too," Bethanne said. Peri did understand.

"Remember when we were little, that day he let us feed the birds in the park," Peri said.

Bethanne nodded. "And one landed on your hand but not on mine."

"I remember sitting there," Peri said, "watching Birdman, seeing how still he kept his hand. I promised myself I wouldn't move even if the bird hurt me. But you—" Peri gave her throaty laugh. "Bethanne, every time a bird started to land on your hand, you yanked it back. You scared the poor things away."

"I *didn't* move," Bethanne protested.

Peri's head nodded up and down. "Yes, you did. Even Birdman laughed, watching those poor confused sparrows."

Bethanne grabbed the book from Peri. "It wasn't funny. I went home and cried because I didn't get a bird."

"Oh, Bethanne," Peri said, shaking her head. "The birds wanted you, you just didn't want them enough." Taking Lissa's hand, Peri leaned close to her. "Lissa, they found roses in Birdman's shack. Did he attack you? Did he?" Peri's eyes widened. "Bethanne!" she cried. "She squeezed my hand. Lissa squeezed my hand. She heard me. She's telling us Birdman's the killer."

The words sent shivers up and down Bethanne's back. "Are you sure?"

Peri placed Lissa's hand in Bethanne's.

"Is it really Birdman, Lissa?" Bethanne said.

There it was—a slight pressure. Bethanne's heart dropped to her stomach.

Not Birdman! she cried silently. Why couldn't it be Ken Kirk?

She looked at Lissa's still form. Suddenly, the

reality of what just happened hit her. "Lissa's getting better. Let's go call Dot."

At home that afternoon, Bethanne told her mother about Lissa's reaction to the question. Her mom patted Bethanne's shoulder. "I know how bad that makes you feel. But maybe she was saying it wasn't Birdman."

Bethanne clutched at the words. She wanted her mom to be right.

"I'm glad Lissa's starting to improve," her mom said. "That's the best news."

"You should have seen Dot when she and her parents got to the hospital," Bethanne said. "When Lissa squeezed Dot's hand, we almost had to pull Dot off the ceiling."

"It looks like all the work you kids have been doing, reading and talking to her, is paying off."

"That's what the doctor said," Bethanne told her.

The excitement about Birdman and Lissa had driven away Bethanne's worry about being fired, but all afternoon her concern grew. In the evening, she watched TV with her parents, one ear listening for the phone. At nine, Dan called and spoke with her mother. Bethanne hovered nearby. "What did he say?" she asked when her mom hung up.

"Birdman's disappeared. No one's had recyclables picked up since last Friday. When Dan contacted Birdman's dad, he said Birdman left a message on his machine on Saturday. Said he was headed for California and would call when he got settled."

"Maybe he's scared, running away because he found those roses," Bethanne's dad said.

"I hope that's so," her mom said, "but . . ." She told him about Lissa's response.

His face reddened with anger. "After everything this town's done for that man! I'd sure like to get my hands on him. Stalking Bethanne, scaring us half to death."

The phone rang again. Her mom picked it up, then handed it to Bethanne. "Ken Kirk." Her mom's eyebrows rose.

Why couldn't Kris have called? Bethanne wondered. I don't want to hear it from him.

She took the receiver. "Hello."

"Hi, Bethanne, sorry to bother you. Kris said she didn't have time to talk with you earlier."

Here it comes.

"The situation is," he went on, "that we're going to Seattle for the weekend."

This didn't sound like being fired. "Kimmie told me," she said.

"I don't want to leave the house empty. We were hoping you would be willing to house-sit from Friday afternoon to Sunday evening. Same pay, of course."

That would be a lot of money! But stay there all night? Well, he wouldn't be there. I can handle it.

She remembered her parents' rule. No place but home in the evenings, because of the Rosekiller. But things had changed. Now, they knew who he was and that he was on his way to California.

"We have a security system," Ken continued, "and Kris said you have a dog. If staying by yourself worries you, you can bring him."

"How about a friend?" Bethanne asked.

"I'd rather not," he said. "You understand."

Bethanne had asked Kris if she could have a

friend over during the mornings. Kris had told her Ken felt there were too many valuable items in the house—paintings, sculptures, computer equipment. He didn't want a lot of people knowing about them. She said Bethanne had gotten the job partly because of her mom. He felt her mother's position on the council suggested Bethanne would be trustworthy.

"I'll have to check with my parents," Bethanne told him.

"That's fine. Tell Kris in the morning."

After hanging up, Bethanne talked the job over with her mom and dad. "The alarm will go off if anyone tries to get in," she said. "If I have problems, I can call you. He's letting Boxer come to keep me company."

At first, her parents argued against her going. They even called Ken back for reassurances about the safety of his home. Finally, to Bethanne's relief, they agreed she could stay the weekend. She had to promise not to tell anyone she would be there.

As she prepared for bed, their arguments against her taking the job came back to worry her. Kirks' house: so isolated on that big lot. The tall trees and bushes: shelter for an intruder prowling around the yard. Being all by herself: Boxer wasn't a guard dog. But she'd be locked in. If anything frightened her, she had the sense to call the police.

So why did the worry hang in her mind? With a sudden rush, she realized what was nagging her. The concern had been there since that afternoon. What if, as her mom suggested, Lissa's hand squeeze meant no? What if it meant Birdman *wasn't* the killer. Then, the Rosekiller was still on the loose.

14

Tuesday morning, Bethanne drove to work. She had to be at the hospital to read to Lissa right after. The day was already warm. Bethanne rode with the front windows rolled down and the radio turned up.

Stopping to take a right off Sixth Street, she glanced in the rearview mirror. A block away, coming toward her, was a red pickup truck.

Like Birdman's. No, that can't be. He's in California.

Still, she squinted, trying to see the left fender. To see if it had a dent like the one on Birdman's truck. The pickup was too far away. She made the turn and moments later looked again. The truck had turned, too. In hopes of getting a peek at the fender and driver, she slowed. The truck stayed a block behind her until she reached Forest Glen Golf Course. As she continued on along the curving road, the truck disappeared from view.

No big deal, she thought. There are lots of red pickups in the world.

Nevertheless, she drove faster, just in case the truck came back. She turned quickly into the Kirks' drive. She glanced around at the tall trees and shrubs that had loomed so large in her imagination the night before. Now, they hid her car and seemed welcoming, more like a protective barrier. When Kimmie opened the door for Bethanne and gave her a hug, some of her concern lifted. "I get to stay home today," Kimmie told her. "Tomorrow, I have to go to the dentist. Do you go to the dentist?"

Bethanne nodded.

"I guess it's okay, then" Kimmie said.

As usual, Ken had left before Bethanne arrived. Kris was waiting in the kitchen, ready to leave.

Bethanne told her she could house-sit.

"I'll tell Ken," was all Kris said. Kissing Kimmie good-bye, she gathered up her briefcase and purse. She left the room without looking at Bethanne.

She's acting like she doesn't want me to do it, Bethanne thought. I thought she'd be pleased.

In the kitchen, Kimmie sat at the counter while Bethanne scrambled her an egg. Kimmie patted the doll beside her. "Heather says she'll stay here with you if you want her to," she told Bethanne.

Bethanne set a plate with egg and toast before her. "I thought Heather wanted to go to the zoo with you."

Kimmie looked at the doll. "Heather says you're our best friend. She doesn't want you to be lonely."

Bethanne smiled at her. "You know what, Kimmie. You and Heather are my best friends, too. You tell Heather not to worry. Boxer's coming to keep me company."

"Heather likes Boxer, too. She wants him to play with her."

"Maybe next week," Bethanne said.

"That's good," Kimmie said, taking a forkful of egg.

After work, Bethanne drove to the hospital to take her turn reading to Lissa. Though Lissa reacted to questions with hand squeezes, she still hadn't opened her eyes. Dot arrived about halfway through Bethanne's time. When one of Lissa's friends relieved Bethanne, she went with Dot to Riverfront.

The hot sun beat down on them as they zigzagged around sunbathers. Now and then, Dot stopped to report to someone on Lissa's progress. Bethanne moved on and found an open space near the river's edge. By that time, sweat was trickling down her back.

She and Dot stripped to bathing suits and raced into the water. The sudden coolness shivered through Bethanne. As her body adjusted to it, the water flowed silkily past her. She swam along the rope against the slow current, back and forth twice before joining Dot, who'd already stretched out on her towel. Bethanne rubbed the water from her hair and lay down, too.

"The Football Four are planning a beach party Saturday night," Dot said. "I think it's to take my mind off Lissa for a while. Want to come? Mark, too." She wiggled her eyebrows up and down.

For a moment, Bethanne thought of telling Dot about the red pickup, but Dot had enough to worry about. She should have a party to look forward to. And she wasn't the Rosekiller's type.

Neither am I! Bethanne wanted to scream.

She hadn't expected to need an excuse for the weekend so fast. "I can't," she said, groping for a reason. "I have to . . . go to my grandma's. She's had a bad cold, and my dad wants to check on her." The last part was true anyway.

"That's too bad. But at least your grandmother's not like mine."

The words reminded Bethanne of the Kirks'

discussion about Mrs. Talbot. "How did your night with her go?" she asked. "Before Lissa got hurt, I mean."

Dot rolled over. "My grandmother was really out of it. She kept ranting about how Ken Kirk's stealing her money. Said if my grandpa were alive it never would have happened. Even my dad couldn't settle her down. Finally, he agreed to call in someone to look over the Kirks' books this week."

"Do the Kirks know about that?" Bethanne sat up and began rubbing suntan lotion on her legs, remembering how just last week she'd hated its coconut aroma. That memory brought a thought of Mark. She hid her smile so Dot wouldn't think Bethanne was laughing at Mrs. Talbot.

"She'd already told Ken Kirk she was going to get someone," Dot said. "Dad was real upset. He said if they were stealing from her, she'd given them a chance to fix the books. Make everything look okay. Then she got mad at Dad for not watching out for her. Like she hasn't been bragging about how much money the Kirks have been making for her over the last four years. After that, we came home to find Lissa gone. Great night, huh?"

"Your poor dad," Bethanne said.

Dot took the lotion from her and rubbed some on Bethanne's back. "I know. He takes good care of Grandmother. He goes to see her every week, makes sure her house is repaired—all that stuff. I hope I don't end up like her."

"No one who giggles like you will ever be a grouchy old lady," Bethanne said.

Dot giggled, then clapped a hand over her mouth. "It is hard to laugh and be mad at the same time. Maybe I should tell my grandmother that."

"Wait until after she finds out about the Kirks," Bethanne said.

"I see what you mean," Dot said, screwing the lotion bottle lid on. "If they are stealing from her, even giggling won't keep her in control."

Wednesday morning, Kimmie went to the dentist. At nine o'clock, Bethanne took the computer list of books to the Valley Public Library. She rode her bike along the shaded town streets. Passing BoTeek with its CLOSED sign, she wondered briefly how Sally was doing.

Peri sure was enjoying her break. Yesterday, she and her mom had gone into Seattle for some big city shopping. Bethanne and Dot spent last evening checking out her new clothes. With all the money Bethanne was making, she'd be able to shop for school clothes in Seattle. She'd already started planning what she'd buy.

Arriving at the library on the edge of town, Bethanne locked her bike and went in. By noon, all but eight of the books were done. She worked for another half hour to complete the job, then went out, blinking in the bright sunlight.

Unlocking her bike, she pulled on her backpack and started home. At the intersection of B and Second, she looked both ways to turn. Down the block toward A street, a red pickup was parked. Could it be the one that had followed her Tuesday morning? She walked her bike toward it.

Suddenly, tires squealing, the truck pulled away from the curb. Speeding past her, the pickup turned right on B. Mouth open, she stared after the truck with its dented left fender. Its driver was wearing a black coat and dark cap.

15

The warm sunlight couldn't stop Bethanne's chills. Her heart thumped hard.

Birdman? Here?

She'd read suspense stories where things like this happened. She always got mad when the main character dismissed the event as unimportant. Then, he or she would go off alone to the deserted mansion or the empty house or the park at midnight. And for sure something terrible would happen. Anyone with a brain bigger than a pea would have more sense.

She had a brain bigger than that. She climbed on her bike and headed for the police station.

Dan sat working in his office. When she entered, he leaned back in his chair. He placed his hands behind his head. "You look worried, Bethanne. What's up?"

Sitting down, she told him about the pickup and the driver. "I don't know whether Birdman was looking for me. Maybe seeing him was just coincidence. If it was him," she added. Now, she was beginning to wonder if she'd seen what she thought she'd seen. "I mean maybe he sold the pickup. Or there's another one with a dented fender and I just imagined . . ."

Dan held up his hand. "I haven't had any reports of the truck. My men probably aren't watching as hard since we heard he went to California. And you're right. You could be imagining, but I don't want to take a chance. If this guy is after you, I want to find him before he gets there. Have you told your parents?"

"Not yet."

He stood and paced the small office. "What we need is a place to hide you while we look for him."

Hide me? Like in that old fairy tale—Snow White?

Bethanne had a sudden image of herself dancing through the forest with the seven dwarves. She pressed her hand against her mouth to stop the giggles. If she started laughing, she might not be able to stop.

"I am supposed to house-sit at the Kirks' this weekend," she finally said.

"Out at Forest Glen?"

She nodded. "No one knows I'm going there."

He sat down again. "That might be an answer. I could have one of my guys keep an eye on the house while you're there. What are the times?"

When she told him, he picked up a pen and wrote a brief note. "Meanwhile," he said, "we'll scour the city for the truck. It's bright enough people should notice it."

Bethanne stood. "Thanks, Dan."

"I should thank you," he said. "A lot of kids wouldn't have the sense to come see me."

She thought for a moment. "I guess nobody wants to seem like a baby, needing to be taken care of."

"Being cautious is a whole lot different from

101

being childish," he told her. As she went out the door, he added, "Remember, stay inside at night until we get this resolved."

Bethanne didn't need that warning. And she felt a lot better about the house-sitting, knowing someone would be watching. She pedaled home to tell her mom.

At Dan's suggestion, one of her parents drove Bethanne back and forth to work the next day. On the trips, Bethanne always watched for the red truck. It didn't appear. She checked with Dan, too. None of his officers reported seeing it, either.

After hearing about the truck, her father had been against her staying at the Kirks' for the weekend. He insisted she'd be safer at home. Dan explained over and over why he wanted to keep her hidden. He promised an officer would be watching out for her. All that didn't completely satisfy her dad, but finally he agreed.

"I'll probably take a ride or two out there," he told Bethanne. They were driving home from the Kirks'.

Suddenly, Bethanne felt angry at everyone trying to take care of her. "I'll be safer at the Kirks' than at home," she argued. "He could always climb in my bedroom window."

She immediately wished she hadn't said that. Her dad's response was that she had to keep her window locked at all times.

"It's summer, Daddy. I'll die of the heat."

Another wrong thing to say. "You're not going to die of anything if I can help it," he snapped.

She flounced out of the car and went in to complain to her mom.

"Bethanne," her mom said, "he's—we're both terrified about this. He doesn't mean to treat you like a child. Remember, three girls your age have been killed and one hurt very badly. That's not something to take any chances with."

"But I'm not taking a chance," Bethanne protested. "I'm doing what Dan says to."

"You're sure you feel okay about going out there."

"I'm a little scared. I'm a little scared here, too. But at least he won't know I'm there." Bethanne sighed. "I just wish it wasn't Birdman."

Her mom hugged her. "I wish it wasn't anyone."

Friday afternoon at four, Bethanne's mother drove her and Boxer to the Kirks'. Both Ken's and Kris's cars sat in the driveway. Kimmie was helping Ken put suitcases in the trunk of his car.

Bethanne's mom got out to say hello to him. His smile bared his teeth as he shook her hand. Bethanne shuddered. She didn't even like him touching her mom. Bethanne's fingers went to her lucky earring. Right then, she felt like she needed it more than ever.

Kimmie, in a ruffly pink dress and patent leather buckle shoes, rushed to Bethanne. The little girl stopped and stood face-to-face with Boxer, who sat by Bethanne.

"Hi, Boxer," Kimmie said. "I'm going to the zoo."

Boxer licked her cheek.

Kimmie stared at him. "Why did he do that?"

Laughing, Bethanne rubbed the moisture from Kimmie's face. "That's how dogs kiss."

103

Kimmie stuck out her tongue. She leaned toward Boxer, then pulled back. "Will he feel bad if I don't kiss him?"

"I think he'd rather have you scratch him behind the ears," Bethanne said.

Her mom joined them. "This is my mother," Bethanne told Kimmie.

Face serious, Kimmie studied her.

"You look pretty," she told Kimmie.

"This is my best dress." Kimmie whirled, spinning her skirt out. "I can't wear it to the zoo. Mama said it might get dirty. Will it get dirty, Bethanne?"

"Your mom's right," Bethanne said.

"I thought so," Kimmie said, whirling around again.

After Bethanne unloaded her bag, her mother backed the car out of the driveway. Kris came from the house. She nodded to Bethanne, then climbed in her own car. Even the short look Bethanne had of her, Bethanne could see Kris's reddened eyes. Maybe she and Ken had had a fight.

"Bethanne," Ken said, "I need to show you things inside."

Not alone, Bethanne thought.

Taking Kimmie's hand and Boxer's leash, she followed Ken in. He stopped in the entry and explained how to operate the security system. "All the windows and doors are locked," he said. "When this is set, if one is opened, the alarm goes off. The signal goes directly to the police department."

Should she tell him about the officer who would be checking on her during the night? Better not. Ken had asked her not to say anything about her being there.

104

"There's something else," he said, "in the family room."

With Kimmie and Boxer, Bethanne continued to that room. As she entered, her eyes immediately went to the small gun on the coffee table. Ken picked up the weapon.

"In case everything fails," he said, holding it out.

Bethanne recoiled, as though it were a striking snake. She didn't even want to touch the thing.

He pointed it toward the kitchen. "Nothing to it. Just aim and pull the trigger." Glancing at Kimmie, he set the gun on the high mantel, well out of her reach.

Kimmie, who'd been talking to Boxer, said, "Bethanne, Mama and I got you the movies you wanted to watch." She pointed to a stack of four videotapes on top of the TV.

Bethanne was relieved by the change of subject. She just wanted to get away from this man. Her skin was beginning to crawl.

"And," Kimmie continued, "I helped make chocolate chip cookies for you." She grinned. "I ate one, too, but just a little one."

"Like you," Bethanne said, ruffling Kimmie's fine hair. Not looking at Ken, she took Kimmie and Boxer back outside.

Bethanne buckled Kimmie into her car seat in Kris's car. They were taking both cars. Ken had appointments all day Saturday. Kris needed her car to get to the zoo.

"Have a good time," Bethanne told Kimmie. "Say hello to the nelephants for me."

"I love you, Bethanne," Kimmie said.

Bethanne hugged her again. "I love you, too."

Kris looked around. "Thanks, Bethanne." Her voice was choked. "I'm sor—"

Ken slammed the car door on her words. He climbed into his car. "We'll see you Sunday evening," he told Bethanne.

Shutting the car's back door, Bethanne looked through the glass at Kris. She stared ahead, her eyes shiny.

16

Bethanne waved to Kimmic until the car was out of sight. Then, Bethanne picked up her bag and, with Boxer, went back into the house. He followed her to the guest bedroom where she changed into her bathing suit.

A few minutes later, she lay on a lounge chair beside the pool. A plate of chocolate chip cookies and a can of pop sat on the table next to her. The stereo was blasting. She waved the Agatha Christie paperback Peri had loaned her.

"This is the life, huh, Boxer?" she said.

Boxer, lying in the shade of bushes along the patio, wagged his tail.

"I wish Mark could be here," she said, tossing Boxer a cookie.

Maybe someday, she'd have a house like this. She and Mark. She pictured the parties they'd have. Peri and her boyfriend, John; Dot; Lissa; the Football Four.

Would they still be around? How much would things change? Just not Mark and me, please, she thought.

He'd spent every evening the past week with her, at home. They'd watched movies, played cards, barbecued, and just sat and talked. He told her his mom died a year ago, and his dad took her death very hard. To get away from the memories, he'd packed Mark up and moved from a town in Oregon. The town Mark had lived in all his life.

"Trouble is," Mark said, "some of those memories let me hold on to her. Here there's nothing."

Bethanne had felt so bad for him. She thought about Valley, her friends, her house. Her great-grandfather had built it. Each generation had added to and changed it to suit. She slept in the bedroom her grandmother Anne had. What would it be like to leave all this?

"Anytime you want to talk about her, you can," she said.

"I knew you'd understand," he told her.

That was when he'd kissed her for the first time. The kiss had felt so natural, she hadn't worried at all about kissing him right. And when he stopped, she'd kissed him. She closed her eyes, remembering the warmth of him.

They'd discussed other things, too, like the environment and rock groups and colleges. Just the thought of his going away made her feel cold inside. But his suggestion they go to the same school helped. He wanted to be with her, too.

Smiling at the thought, she rolled over onto her stomach and opened the book.

When the sun slid behind one of the tall trees, Bethanne shivered from the sudden coolness. Picking up the cookie plate, book, and pop can, she called Boxer and went inside.

Long shadows were stretching across the patio and pool, giving the yard a slightly sinister look. She searched the bushes for signs of movement. Everything was still. Locking the sliding door, pulling the curtain to keep out the dark, made the house feel a little less creepy. Boxer followed her to the entry to set the alarm

"All safe," she told him, when the lights went on.

She wished she could call Mark. Outside of her family and the police, he was the only person who knew where she was. She hadn't liked the idea of telling him a lie about the weekend. She could trust him to keep the secret. Besides, she figured she'd get lonely. Talking on the phone would make time pass faster.

She checked her watch. Six-thirty. Mark and his dad were going out for dinner and movie. They'd be home about ten.

After changing into jeans and a T-shirt, she returned to the kitchen. She set a Mexican TV dinner in the microwave. When Boxer barked three times, she jumped. The doorbell rang. He hurried with her to the entry where she peeked out the peephole. A uniformed man stood on the porch. She'd seen him once at the police station.

Dan had told her the man would check when he first came on duty. She had a code word, "cool," to use when he asked how things were if something were wrong.

"How's everything?" he asked through the door.

"Fine," she said.

"Do you want me to come in and look around?" he asked.

It would be reassuring to have him check all the rooms, just in case. Then Bethanne remembered the suggestion that the Rosekiller might be a cop. She wouldn't take a chance.

"No thanks. I've got the alarm set," she said.

"Good," he told her. "I'll be keeping an eye on you tonight."

She returned to the kitchen and opened a can of dog food for Boxer. He kept her company at dinner.

This is really boring, she thought as she cleaned up. She peeked out the curtain. Dusk had fallen. The day was quickly fading into night. She plopped onto the couch. Might as well watch a movie.

She chose one of the lighthearted films she'd asked Kris for. After setting it up, she opened another can of pop and a bag of chips, then settled down to watch. Boxer climbed up beside her and helped her eat the chips.

The movie had gone on about an hour when Boxer barked. At the same time, the curtains swayed. The house creaked. Boxer jumped from the couch.

"What is it, boy?" she said.

Boxer whined, barked once more, and looked toward the entry.

She stopped the movie and listened. No sounds. Still, it was creepy, the way that curtain moved. And the creaking. Houses did have drafts, didn't they?

"I know what you heard," she finally told him. "The patrol car. Don't worry, he's keeping us safe. I hope." She touched her lucky earring.

She patted the couch pillow, but he remained gazing out. Watching the movie, she hadn't noticed how dark the room had grown. She switched on a table lamp.

Maybe she should call Mark. She wanted the

comfort of talking to someone. She looked at her watch. Nine-thirty.

Darn. Not yet.

Moving around, she realized the room had cooled. She rubbed her bare arms. "Be right back," she told Boxer and rushed to the bedroom for a sweatshirt.

From down the hall, she heard him yelp again. Now her goose bumps weren't from cool air.

You're being silly, she told herself. You're all locked in.

Nevertheless, she stayed close to the wall and crept toward the family room. Eyes watchful, ears straining, she edged into it, then stopped.

A man in a long black coat and watch cap came toward her. His face looked twisted, deformed. In his gloved hands, he held a rope and a red rose.

"No, Birdman, don't!" she screamed over Boxer's barks.

Everything went black.

"Boxer, stop!"

Bethanne struggled through layers of blackness. She was so hot. And her face was sticky from Boxer's licking. She pushed his head away. The movement sent a pain stabbing through hers. She gasped, then choked on her breath. That noise! That smell! The heat! Her eyes sprang open.

For a moment, she stared, trying to figure out where she was. Just for a moment. Flames danced around her. Smoke hazed the room. She lifted her head. Dizziness whirled it back down. She moaned and Boxer whined. He pulled on her sweatshirt with his teeth.

Ignoring the pain in her head, she scooted toward the sliding glass door. Her quick breaths were into her sleeve. At the door, she yanked aside the curtain. She struggled up, stretched for the handle.

Dizzy. So dizzy. Can't pass out now.

Her fingers found the lock. Pushed. Pushed again.

Click.

She fell back to the floor. Coughing. Choking. Hurts so bad. Can't breathe. Get out. Hurry!

She slid the door open. The rush of air fueled the fire. It flared up behind her, crackling loudly.

Something was missing, something should have happened. She dragged herself over the sill. That didn't matter. All she wanted was air that didn't hurt to breathe. And the pool. Cool water on her face.

Before she could travel farther, the dizziness overwhelmed her.

"Bethanne, wake up."

Mark's voice. Where was she? Outside. The cool air smelled smoky. A barbecue? Picnic?

Sirens! She heard sirens. And fire crackling. Felt its heat. Everything tumbled into place. The fire. Escaping. Boxer.

"Boxer," she moaned. "Where's Boxer?"

A bark answered her question. Even talking sent knives through her head. She reached to the pain. Her hair was sticky.

She forced her eyes open. She lay under a tree beyond the patio. Mark sat beside her. Flickering light from the fire showed a man leaning against the tree.

"Don't talk," Mark said. "Dad"—he gestured to the man—"says you've got a bad head injury."

She stared at him.

"What am I doing here?" Mark asked her question. "I was worried about you," he said. "So after the movie, Dad and I drove over just to check. Good thing. You'd barely gotten outside before you passed out. The fire was creeping up on you. Poor Boxer. He was about crazy."

The sirens stopped. "Sounds like the big guys are here," Mark said.

His father moved away from the tree. "I'll get help."

Almost immediately, two men came with a stretcher. They checked her over, then loaded her on and placed her in the aid truck. She waved a two-finger good-bye to Mark as they closed the door, then closed her eyes and let the darkness take her.

She woke in a hospital bed. Light shining in the window told her it was daytime. Her parents and Dan, in his uniform, sat beside the bed. She looked at the bottle slowly dripping liquid into her arm, then felt her head. A bandage covered it.

"Just like Lissa," she said.

Tears filled her mom's eyes. "You have a concussion."

"Bethanne," her dad said. His face was twisted, tormented. "We should have been there checking on you, but your grandmother called us. She was having trouble breathing. We had to get her to the doctor."

"Poor Grandma," Bethanne said. "Is she all right?"

He nodded. "But we should have been checking on you," he said again.

"I'll be okay," Bethanne said. "My head doesn't hurt nearly as much as it did last night."

Her parents and Dan exchanged concerned looks.

"What's the matter?" she asked.

"Do you remember what happened?" her father said.

The question brought the horror back. She shuddered with the memory. "The fire? Yeah.

Noise and heat and being scared. And Boxer. He woke me up."

"How about before that? Before you passed out."

Bethanne closed her eyes. Before . . . before she passed out. Something had struck her. And right before that . . . Birdman. The thought, so sudden, brought pain and lights flashing in front of her eyes.

"It was Birdman. He had a rope and a rose. He was coming for me. But I didn't pass out. Something hit me." She paused. "What happened to Birdman? Was he in the fire?"

Her father stood and paced to the window. "Birdman wasn't there, Bethanne."

"You mean he got out?"

"No, he wasn't there."

"Daddy, a man came at me, dressed like Birdman. Who else could it be?"

"What about the gun?" Dan asked.

"The gun?" She frowned. "The one Ken showed me? It was on the mantel. I never even touched it. Why are you asking me all this?" Bethanne's heart beat hard. Something was going on she didn't understand.

Dan took her hand. "Bethanne, a man was found in the fire. He'd been shot, and we think it was with that gun. But it wasn't Birdman. It was Ken Kirk."

18

"Ken Kirk!" The name exploded in Bethanne's head. "He was in Seattle."

"His wife said he forgot a briefcase and drove back for it."

Poor Kris, Bethanne thought. And Kimmie. He was a creep, but how awful.

"Did Birdman shoot him?" she asked.

Dan gently took her hand. "Bethanne, last night we ran a powder check on your hands," he said. "It tells if you've recently fired a gun. It's something we had to do." His tone was apologetic.

"You don't have to worry about me," Bethanne said. "I never touched it."

Dan cleared his throat. "The test showed you fired one, Bethanne."

She looked wildly from her mom to her dad. This couldn't be happening. "You think I shot Ken Kirk! No, that's not right. I didn't. I didn't even see him. And I could never do that. I told you what happened. Birdman was there, then I got knocked out."

Her head pounded so hard she couldn't even think. "Tell him, Dad," she pleaded.

"I think you better go, Dan," her dad said. "The doctor said she needs rest and quiet."

Dan stood. "I'm sorry, Bethanne. We'll get to the bottom of this when you feel better."

As he left the room, her mom rang for a nurse. "Why won't he listen?" Bethanne asked. The pain in her head throbbed with her words.

"The police think Ken came into the house and scared you, so you shot him," her dad said. "Then you passed out, and your head hit the coffee table when you fell. That knocked the lamp onto some papers, starting the fire. The situation was so traumatic, you've blocked it all out."

"But I do remember what happened," she said. "And I know Ken. It couldn't have been him." A picture slowly formed in her head of Birdman approaching her, his face twisted. "I couldn't tell the face for sure," she said, "but he was dressed like Birdman. Why would Ken do that?"

A nurse came in.

"She needs to rest," Bethanne's mom said. Her eyes were worried.

"How's your head?" the nurse asked.

"Hurts," Bethanne replied, "a lot."

The nurse injected something into the tube. "This'll help," she told her.

Her parents stood. Her mom kissed Bethanne's forehead.

"You sleep," she said. "And don't worry. We believe you. We'll make sure things work out."

People think I'm a murderer, Bethanne thought, and then her thoughts slipped away.

She woke to the sound of dinner being wheeled in. The server raised her bed so that she sat up. The initial dizziness faded, and to her surprise, she was able to eat the spaghetti, green beans, and fruit compote. As she finished, Peri, Dot, and Mark walked in.

"I must look terrible," Bethanne said, just as Dot said, "Bethanne, you look terrible." At Mark and Peri's surprised looks, Dot clapped a hand over her mouth. "I'm sorry," she said. "I always say the wrong thing. It's just that usually you look so perfect." She hugged Bethanne.

Despite the pain the embrace caused, Bethanne hugged her back. Dot had never paid her a compliment like that before.

"She looks great considering what she went through," Mark said.

"I think you look wonderful," Peri told her. "At least, you're alive."

"The newspaper said you might have killed Ken Kirk," Dot said. "Did you?"

"Dot!" Mark and Peri said together.

At the same moment, Bethanne blurted out, "No!" How could anyone have written something like that? she wondered.

This time, Dot blushed. "I did it again, didn't I? Well, I didn't think you did, but I wouldn't have blamed you. Some guy surprising you like that."

"It wasn't him," Bethanne told her. "It was Birdman. First he walked in, then someone knocked me out. I don't know what happened after that." She was already tired of telling the story.

Mark took her hand. She held on tight. "I didn't even touch the gun. Someone else killed him."

"Maybe his wife," Dot said, "to collect the million-dollar insurance."

Was that why Kris was so upset yesterday? Bethanne wondered. *Because she planned to kill Ken?*

118

"She had Kimmie with her," Bethanne argued. "How could she have done it?"

"They were at a hotel, right?" Mark asked. "Hotels have baby-sitters."

"How long do you have to stay in here?" Peri asked.

"Just until tomorrow, I hope," Bethanne said.

"Good, because it looks like we've got some detective work to do."

Dot's eyes lit up. "Like in Nancy Drew books," she said.

"Sure," Peri told her, "but this is Bethanne, for real. We have to get her out of trouble."

Mark and Peri pulled up chairs. Dot sat on the bed, her feet dangling over the side.

"Start at the beginning," Peri told Bethanne.

Bethanne told them about Mark finding the rose by the tree, then she and her mom finding more roses at Birdman's shack, about being followed by Birdman and seeing his truck in town. She continued with what happened Friday night, from the time her mom dropped her off.

"Whose fingerprints were on the gun?" Peri wanted to know.

"How did Kris tell it was Ken if he was all burned?" Dot asked.

"How could Birdman get in if the alarm was on?" Peri said.

Mark took a pencil from his pocket. He pulled the placemat from the dinner tray and began writing on the back of the paper. "The questions," he explained. "We have to get answers."

"Did the Kirks have a baby-sitter in Seattle?" "What did they fight about?" "Was Ken stealing money from my grandmother?" "Who else might want to kill Ken?" "How did Bethanne get gunpowder on her fingers?"

The questions came so fast, twice Mark had to stop everyone so he had time to write.

"I think we should go out to the Kirks' house," Mark suggested. "If the police don't believe you, Bethanne, they won't be looking for clues about Birdman. Or anyone else. Maybe we can find something."

"I'm not sure I can go," Bethanne said. Not that she wanted to. Just the thought of the house made her stomach roll.

"No need," Peri said, laughing. "You've got three super sleuths to do your legwork."

Dot giggled. "Peri, you sound like a real detective."

"Thanks, Watson," Peri said.

"That's not my name," Dot told her.

Peri's eyebrows rose. "Sherlock Holmes, remember?"

"Oh, right," Dot said.

A nurse came in to say Bethanne needed rest. "It sounds like you've stayed long enough," she told them.

Dot headed down the hall to see Lissa. Lissa had started making sounds and moving around. The doctor said there was a chance she could wake up at any time.

Mark kissed Bethanne good-bye. She held him tight. "Thanks for believing me," she said.

"Believing you! I'm going to clear your name, pardner."

"Mark" she said, imitating Dot's voice, "you

sound like a real cowboy." As he started to speak, she held up a hand. "Don't you dare call me Old Paint."

19

After Mark, Peri, and Dot left, Bethanne lay back, exhausted. Talking to her friends had held off the fear. Now, it rushed in. She was a murder suspect, and she hadn't killed anyone.

Then how did you get gunpowder on your fingers? a small voice asked.

She closed her mind to the thought. She could never kill anyone, never.

What if he was going to kill you?

I would have run, locked myself in the bedroom, called the police. Or opened the glass door and set off the alarm. Wait, I opened the door and the alarm didn't ring. Someone turned it off.

Ken.

But she hadn't killed him. She couldn't have. She was knocked out.

And the gunpowder on your fingers?

She groaned. This was going around in circles. All she knew for sure was that she was innocent.

Innocent until proven guilty.

Wasn't that how it was supposed to be? But the way Dan had sounded, everything pointed to her guilt. Murderers went to jail. Sweat broke out on her forehead. She didn't want to go to jail.

Why was this happening?

Someone set me up. The thought came suddenly. Someone killed Ken and tried to make it look like I did it. Tried to kill me, too. If I had died, there would be no one to tell what really happened.

If Mark hadn't shown up . . . but he did. So stop thinking about that, she told herself.

She knew she'd set the alarm right. The lights had gone on, showing it was working. Birdman must have snuck in somehow when she was by the pool. Then only the front door had been locked. She should have let that cop check the house.

Later, Ken walked in on Birdman, so Birdman killed him and framed her. He didn't know she'd get out of the burning house and tell that he was there. That's the only explanation that made sense. Dan had to believe her. And if he didn't? What was she going to do?

Her head began to throb. She couldn't think straight anymore. She pushed the button for the nurse.

The next morning, the pain in her head had lessened to a dull ache. After checking her, the doctor insisted she stay another day. "It's still a bad concussion," she told Bethanne. "I want to keep an eye on you."

Dan arrived with her parents after lunch. Bethanne showed him the list of questions Mark had made.

"We'll start from the top," Dan said. "Fingerprints. Bethanne's were the only ones on the gun. Kris identifying Ken? His body was pretty burned by the time we got to him. She recognized the gold watch, ring, and neck chain he wore. We went even further, using dental records. The guy never had a cavity. Neither did the man in the fire." Dan slapped his hand to his cheek. "When I think of all the time I spent in the dentist's chair . . ." He stopped. "Sorry. Didn't mean to get off the subject. The last question's about Birdman's getting into the house without setting off the alarm. That's based on your story, Bethanne. You said you had the alarm on. Ken deactivated it before he came in."

"When I got the sliding door open, no alarm went off," she told him. "So Ken did come in—after I passed out. See, I figure Birdman got in before I set the alarm, then Ken walked in on Birdman when he was going to attack me. Birdman shot him and made it look like I did it. He thought I'd die in the fire."

"It could have happened that way," Bethanne's mom said.

Dan sighed. "Then where was Birdman's truck? My deputy never saw it. He checked the Kirks' place four separate times that night."

"Maybe Birdman walked there," Bethanne said.

"Someone would have seen him. It was Friday night. Even people in Forest Glen come home from work. Birdman wouldn't take that chance."

"He could have hidden in the bushes all day," Bethanne said, "waiting for a chance to get into the house." She thought a moment. "It doesn't make sense—waiting until after nine to attack me."

Dan sat up in the chair. "What do you mean, after nine?"

"That's when I saw him."

"Are you sure?"

"I'd just checked my watch," Bethanne told him. "Why, what difference does it make?"

124

"My deputy's log said that Ken's car was in the drive at seven-thirty."

"That's crazy," Bethanne said.

"Maybe you aren't remembering right," he said. "You had a nasty head bang." He squeezed her hand. "I'm sorry. There's nothing I'd like better than to find a way to prove you didn't do this." He shook his head. "We'll have an inquest next Thursday to look into the death. Maybe something will come to light, but . . ."

"But you don't think so," Bethanne said. "You think I shot Ken, don't you?"

"But if it doesn't," he continued, "whether I like it or not, you're all I have."

"Wait a minute, Dan," her dad said. His anger showed in his clenched jaw.

"Jack," Dan said, "I've got three girls dead by the Rosekiller and no one caught. And now another killing. I'm getting a lot of heat from the mayor to solve this case. He wants me to file charges. I'm holding him off, hoping something shows up to prove Bethanne didn't do it. But it's got to happen fast. So far, I don't have anything like that."

"It's okay, Dad," Bethanne said. Blaming Dan didn't solve the problem. "Maybe the answers to those questions will give you some ideas," she told Dan.

Standing, he waved the paper. "I'll let you know what I learn."

"One other question," Bethanne's mom said. "Why would Birdman keep after Bethanne? That's what doesn't make sense to me."

After Dan left, her parents tossed around the information he'd given them. Bethanne only partly listened to their talk. She was trying to figure out why some of the discussion with him bothered her. Her mom's mention of the gun brought back a memory of Ken aiming it toward the kitchen.

"The gun should have Ken's fingerprints on it, too," she told her parents.

"Maybe Birdman wiped them off."

"Why? He had gloves on."

"Could someone else have been there?" her mom asked.

"That's it!" Bethanne's shout sent pain stabbing through her head. "I knew something else didn't work. Who knocked me out?"

Her mom laid a hand on her shoulder. "You're not supposed to get excited. Let us worry about these things."

"We better let you rest," her dad said, standing. "I'll call Dan and add those questions to his list."

They left and Bethanne curled up to take a nap, but her mind whirled. The inquest on Thursday was to decide what happened and who might have done it. She knew that from reading mystery novels. Tomorrow was Monday. She had only three days to find out what really went on.

After dinner, Peri, Dot, and Mark showed up. Bethanne filled them in on what she'd learned.

"We went to the Kirks' house," Dot said. "It had a yellow tape all around the yard that said we should stay away." She giggled. "It didn't stop us. One end of the house is all burned. It was so dirty. Black soot everywhere and water from the firemen. The smell was terrible." She wrinkled her nose.

"I wish we'd found something," Mark said, "but I think the cops had gone over the house pretty thoroughly."

"So where do we go next?" Dot asked. "Some-place clean this time, I hope."

"We've got until that inquest on Thursday," Mark said slowly. "I think we should start looking for Birdman."

"He might be on his way to California," Beth-anne said.

"If he's in his truck, the cops'll pick him up," Mark told her. "Besides, your story about seeing him hasn't been in the paper. He may just figure you don't remember, lay low here for a while."

"But where do we look?" Peri asked.

"Parking lots," he said. "Logging roads. Maybe abandoned barns."

"I have to work tomorrow morning," Peri said, "but I'll help after."

"Sally's back?" Bethanne said.

"Yeah. We're opening day after tomorrow. Sally tripped on a stair at her sister's and broke her arm. She wants me to kind of take over the shop, the stocking and heavy stuff. I need to change the window display. I told her I was reading to Lissa, and she offered to take my turn. If you're here tomorrow morning, she might stop in and see you."

"That's a good reason to go home," Bethanne said, laughing. It felt good to laugh for a change.

"I'm taking tomorrow off," Mark told her. "If you do get out, we can drive around looking."

At nine the next morning, the doctor dismissed Bethanne. "No marathon races, no all-night par-ties for a few weeks," the doctor told her.

Bethanne called Mark. "I'm out," she said. "I'll be ready in an hour."

Hanging up, she called her mom and told her. "Mark's picking me up."

"Come right home and rest for a while," her mom said.

"Oh, Mom, the doctor just said to take it easy. Mark's taking me for a ride. I've been inside for days. I need to get out."

"You won't overdo it?"

"If I get tired, I'll come home. I promise."

Her mother sighed. "All right. But not too late."

When the nurse temporarily removed the head wound bandage, Bethanne discovered a section of her hair had been shaved off.

"I look terrible," she moaned.

"It's already growing back," the nurse assured her.

Bethanne touched the shaved part. Tiny bristles. She'd never really liked the color, but it was sure better than no hair at all. She called Peri, pleased to find her still home.

When Bethanne explained the problem, Peri said, "I'll bring you a sun hat."

"Fast!" Bethanne said. "Mark will be here in thirty minutes."

She showered, and with the nurse's help, washed her hair. Her mom had brought clean shorts and a shirt to the hospital the day before. Bethanne pulled them on. As she stroked on mascara, Peri rushed in with a straw sun hat.

"It's my mom's," Peri said.

Bethanne carefully adjusted it to cover the bandage. "I look like I should be out in the fields weeding," she moaned.

"That's what Mom uses it for." Peri's reddening

face suggested held-back laughter. "Leave it off," she told Bethanne. "You'll get more sympathy."

Mark came in. Bethanne waited for his reaction. He hugged her, then rubbed his jaw. "You need a shave," he said, grinning.

The nurse brought a wheelchair. "Hospital policy," she said when Bethanne insisted she'd walk. Mark pushed her and the chair out the door.

"Maybe we should stop and see Lissa," Bethanne said. "I feel bad I haven't been able to read to her."

Peri looked at her watch. "Are you sure? Sally's just started her shift."

"That's okay," Bethanne said. "I'll tell her I feel dizzy after just a minute."

They rode the elevator down to Lissa's floor. The cop waved them in. Mark opened the door.

20

The scene inside Lissa's hospital room was like a tableau: Sally stretched across the head of the bed, Lissa's head hidden beneath the pillow Sally lay on. Sally looked toward the door. Her eyes widened in surprise.

For a moment, everyone stared. Bethanne was the first to speak.

"She's smothering Lissa!" she screamed.

Before Bethanne could leave the chair, Mark grabbed Sally. Sally swung her arm, and the cast caught him in the mouth. He fell back, blood running from his lip.

"Help us!" Bethanne shouted to the cop sitting outside.

Now Peri grappled with Sally. As Mark jumped on the woman's back, Bethanne rushed to pull the pillow off Lissa's face. Lissa was gasping for air.

"What's going on?" The policeman stood at the door.

Peri, Mark, and Sally continued to struggle. Mark's blood spotted Sally's shirt.

"You kids get away from her," the cop shouted.

Mark and Peri jumped back so fast Sally staggered. She glared at the cop. "Arrest them," she said, her voice breathless. "They attacked me."

Everyone started talking at once. A hand grasped Bethanne's. She looked down to see Lissa holding on to her. Lissa's eyes were open!

"Lissa, you're awake!" Bethanne cried.

"It's Sally. The Rosekiller," Lissa croaked out.

Before Bethanne could react, Sally screamed and leaped on the bed. This time, the policeman grabbed her and wrestled her to the floor. He snapped handcuffs on her.

A doctor and nurse hurried into the room. Bethanne stayed by the bed, holding Lissa's hand. Behind her, she heard the cop say, "You have the right to remain silent. Anything you say . . ."

The doctor leaned over Lissa, checking her. "Looks like we got her back," he said finally.

"Tell Dot," she rasped out.

"Sounds like you need some oil," the doctor told her.

Lifting Lissa's head, the nurse gave her a sip of water.

"She'll need to rest," the doctor said.

The nurse helped Mark clean off his lip. "Feels like a balloon," he said, opening and closing his mouth.

Bethanne settled back in the wheelchair. "Let's call Dot."

Once the call was made, and they'd calmed Dot down a little, the three went to the parking lot. They sat in the shade of a tree in the grass strip along the edge.

"I can't believe it," Peri said for about the thousandth time. "Sally, the Rosekiller."

"It kind of makes sense," Bethanne said. She'd been thinking about this since they left Lissa's room. "I mean, the girls she attacked were all like models—young and pretty the way Sally used to be. And look at how mad she got when those women she knew in New York were still modeling. My psychiatric opinion"—Bethanne lifted her chin and stared down her nose—"is that she was jealous and couldn't control it."

Peri nodded. "Do you think she's crazy?"

"I bet she says she is," Mark said.

"Bethanne," Peri said, "if Sally's the Rosekiller, how does Birdman fit in?"

Birdman and Sally had been spinning in Bethanne's head since Lissa's identification. Sally was just interested in models. She wouldn't have been the person with the red rose outside Bethanne's house. Now, the answer to Bethanne's mother's question *Why was Birdman after Bethanne?* was even more important for solving the puzzle of what happened Friday night.

Bethanne had seen movies about persons obsessed by other people. Maybe because of the war that had happened to Birdman. But why all of a sudden, after she'd known him all these years?

Mark stood, his movement interrupting her thoughts. He offered her a hand up. "Let's go find out where Birdman fits."

Peri stood also. "I just realized. I'm out of a job. Darn. I may have to work at my mom's restaurant after all."

"Me, too," Bethanne said. "The drugstore." She shrugged. "Hey, maybe we could trade. I'll work for your mom. You work for my dad."

"Not a bad idea," Peri said.

After leaving Peri, Bethanne lay back in the car seat. Mark drove to the town's parking lots. When they'd checked them with no luck, he stopped to pick up hamburgers. He and Bethanne ate as they drove out to farm country to inspect abandoned sheds and barns. The sun warmed the car and Bethanne fought to stay awake, but finally she dropped off.

Mark's excited voice woke her. She gazed around, trying to get her bearings. They'd left Valley. Mark had parked on a pull off on the road high above the river. Through the open car window, she heard the faint rush of the water below.

"I drove up here to check logging roads." Mark spoke through her window. "I stopped to stretch." He opened the car door for her. "Got something to show you." His swollen lip twisted his grin.

Holding her hand, he led her to the edge of the cliff overlooking the river. He pointed down. Partially buried in underbrush far below was a pile of twisted red metal.

"It might be Birdman's truck," he told her. "I hope he's not in it."

"Let's go tell Dan," she said.

Half an hour later, they left the police station. Dan had sent two deputies out to investigate the wreck. He promised to call Bethanne as soon as he had information about it. Mark dropped her off at home.

Inside, Boxer rushed to greet her. She joined her parents, who were eating dinner on the patio. Sitting, she threw her arms around Boxer.

"You're such a good dog," she said.

He licked her face.

"I gave him steak for dinner last night," her dad said, "just saying thank you."

Her mom studied her face. "You look exhausted." She poured Bethanne a glass of lemonade.

Bethanne took a long drink of the cold liquid. She sprawled back in the chair. Her head hurt. "I've never been so tired. Or confused."

She told them all about Sally and finding the wrecked truck.

"Why didn't you call me earlier and tell me?" her mom asked.

"I'm sorry," Bethanne said. "There was so much going on. And we wanted to get out of there."

Her mom frowned. "More pieces of the puzzle, but I don't know where they fit."

"Sally's the Rosekiller?" her dad said. "She killed those girls, and you've been in her shop. That close." He shook his head. "That's a frightening thought."

"Peri, too," her mom added. "And she's the type the Rosekiller went after."

"Dan says serial killers don't usually kill the people they know," Bethanne told them.

"She knew Lissa," her dad argued.

"Just to say hello," Bethanne said. "Now I'm glad I spent a lot of time in BoTeek talking to Sally."

Her dad patted her shoulder. "Me, too."

Her mom brought her a plate holding a barbecued hamburger and carrot sticks. Bethanne nibbled at a carrot. Tiredness weighed heavy in her bones.

"I can't eat," she said. "I'm going to bed."

The doorbell and Boxer's barks woke Bethanne the next morning. From the entry, she heard her mom and Dan talking. After pulling on shorts and a shirt, she went to the kitchen. Dan and her mother looked up from the table where they sat over coffee.

Bethanne joined them. She had so many questions to ask Dan—about Birdman, about Sally—but was almost afraid to start. The more things that happened, the more she seemed to be guilty of killing Ken.

Her mother pushed a plate holding several glazed doughnuts to her.

"Dan's treat," her mom said.

Bethanne took one, setting it on a napkin. She licked her fingers.

"I just told your mom the truck was Birdman's," Dan said. "He wasn't in it."

Bethanne gave a relieved sigh. Despite everything, she didn't want Birdman to die.

"How did the truck get there, then?" she asked.

He shrugged. "We don't know. One strange thing. It had been wiped clean of fingerprints."

"Why would Birdman do that? And why would he wreck his truck?"

"I wish I knew," he said. "This straightforward case is getting more complicated by the hour."

Bethanne understood what he meant. Every time you thought you knew something for sure, an event happened to change your mind. Like Sally being the Rosekiller instead of Birdman.

"What about Sally?" she asked.

"Sally?" he said, his voice incredulous. "First she babbles about saving those girls from going through what she did in the modeling world. Next she's wailing she had to get rid of the young models who were taking away her job. I think she thought she could wipe out the next generation of models." With a finger, he made circles by his ear. "If you ask me, she's nutty as a fruitcake. I'm just glad you

135

kids stopped her." He paused for a drink of coffee. "I should have trusted my instincts on this, instead of running all over looking for Birdman."

"What do you mean?" Bethanne asked.

"The red roses. Wrong color. Pink roses were left with the murdered girls." He pulled a paper from his pocket. "I've got some answers to your questions."

Bethanne took a bite of doughnut. Here it came. Maybe her last chance to figure out this whole thing.

"The Kirks did have a baby-sitter in Seattle," he said. "Mrs. Kirk said when they went out to dinner Ken discovered he'd forgotten the briefcase. She went to a movie while he drove to Valley."

"Can they prove it?" Bethanne's mom asked.

"No one at the restaurant remembers seeing them, but it's a very busy place. Mrs. Kirk did describe the movie. It's one that showed in Valley last week, so that doesn't mean much."

"It means she doesn't have an alibi," Bethanne said.

"We're considering that." He smiled at her. "Your next question was about their fight before they left. Mrs. Kirk said nothing like that happened. She'd slammed her finger in the door. Her eyes were red from tears over that."

"She's lying," Bethanne said. "I saw how upset she was."

"Maybe. But even if they had a fight, there's no reason it had to have anything to do with the murder."

The last word turned Bethanne's blood to ice.

"The problem about Ken embezzling money is more complex. Mrs. Talbot hired a man to go over the books. Since this was Ken Kirk's account, Mrs.

Kirk asked for some time to get it in order." He leaned back in his chair. "Now, as to who might want to kill Kirk . . . the answer is very interesting. We learned this morning that he had four one-million-dollar life insurance policies. All payable to his wife."

"Four!" Bethanne gasped. With that kind of money Kris wouldn't have to shoplift. She and Kimmie would have everything they wanted. More, probably. But life insurance cost money to buy. Why would he want to spend that much?

"That sounds like a motive to me," her mom said. "A fight. No alibi. And she had a car. She could have driven back, too."

"Yeah," Bethanne added, her heart racing. "Knocked me on the head, killed Ken, and rushed back to Seattle." Though it was hard to imagine Kris standing up to Ken. Or Ken letting her. Bethanne had gotten the feeling he could talk Kris into anything.

"My deputy didn't see her car at their house that night," Dan said.

His words were like a splash of cold water.

"And it wouldn't explain the last question," he went on, "the one about the traces of powder on your hands."

Without thinking, Bethanne rubbed her hands on her shorts, as though trying to scrape off the evidence. When she saw him watching her, she stopped. She picked up the doughnut to hide her discomfort.

"There has to be an answer," she said. "An answer besides me, I mean."

21

After Dan left, Bethanne ate another doughnut, then opened the morning newspaper. She needed to think about something beside Birdman and murder. She thumbed through the pages, looking for the comics. She stopped abruptly, her heart in her throat. Ken Kirk's obituary. She knew she shouldn't read it, but she couldn't stop herself. The words "survived by his wife, Kris, and daughter, Kimmie" sent pain stabbing into her chest.

It's real, she thought. Up until now, I almost didn't believe it. Could I have killed him? What if I did?

The notice said the funeral was Wednesday morning. Should she go? She wanted to tell Kris how sorry she felt and that she hadn't killed Ken. But she couldn't do that there. And what about Kimmie? Had they told her Bethanne shot her dad? The thought twisted in her stomach, made her head spin. She lay it down on the paper.

Then her mom's hands were kneading Bethanne's shoulders, draining away some of the tension.

"We'll get through this," her mom said.

Tears stung Bethanne's eyes. She blinked them back. She couldn't give in to self-pity now.

"I just wish I knew where to start," she said.

Her mother put a pencil and paper on the table. "Write everything down. Maybe you'll see something you've missed."

Bethanne thought for a minute, then picked up the pencil and wrote:

1. *Someone in yard, leaves rose*
2. *Lissa attacked*
3. *Birdman disappears*
4. *Find roses at Birdman's*
5. *His truck follows me*
6. *At Kirks' Kris has been crying*
7. *Set security alarm about 6:00*
8. *Cop sees Ken's car at 7:30*
9. *Boxer barks about 9:30*
10. *Birdman comes in*
11. *I get hit on the head*

She put her hand up and touched the bandage.

12. *Ken is killed*
13. *I escape from the fire, alarm doesn't go off*
14. *We find Birdman's truck*

She read down the list.

"Why would Birdman pretend to be the Rosekiller?" she asked. "Just to scare me? If he wanted to kill me, he could have done it after he murdered Ken. But if he wasn't the Rosekiller, why would he disappear after Lissa's attack?" She tapped the pencil on number eight. "What was Ken doing between seven-thirty and nine-thirty?"

She stared at the page. "This doesn't help!" she

said, throwing down the pencil. Any minute now she was going to give into that self-pity.

The phone rang. Bethanne grabbed up the receiver as though it were a lifeline. Mark said hello.

She blurted out her frustration.

"Dad doesn't need me here," he said. "I'll come right over. Maybe the two of us can make sense of things."

Boxer's barking announced Mark's arrival. When Bethanne let Mark in, he asked, "How long will I have to come here before Boxer gets used to me?"

She laughed. Mark had a way of lifting the shadows. "Probably forever. The only person he never barked at was Birdman."

The words hung in the air, took her breath away.

"Mark," she choked out, "you know what that means?"

Frowning, he shook his head. She grabbed his hand and pulled him into the kitchen. Goose bumps covered her arms. She pointed to the paper lying on the table.

"Look at the first one. 'Someone in yard . . .' Remember how Boxer barked? He doesn't bark at Birdman." Between "1" and "2" she squeezed in the words "Boxer barks." "That means someone else was in the shadows." She read line nine. "'Boxer barks about 9:30.'" She added "Boxer never barks at Birdman," then tapped the paper. "Whoever was in the house wasn't Birdman."

22

"Bethanne," Mark said, "all you've proven is what the cops have been saying."

"No," she said, shaking her head. "They say he wasn't there at all. I say someone dressed up like him was there." She thought back to the night. The memory hadn't faded at all. "That's why his face looked twisted. Because it wasn't his face. Whoever it was probably wore a stocking over it, like a bank robber. So who was it?"

"Someone who could turn off the security system," she said, answering her own question. "Kris. But she's not big enough to look like Birdman. Ken is. So let's say Ken pretended to be Birdman."

"But why?" Mark asked.

Bethanne chewed on the pencil. "In case I lived through the fire. The cops would think just what they do—that I made up the story."

"But why would Ken want to set fire to his house? And who killed him?" Mark said.

"Kris must have come with him. She shot him for the insurance."

Sighing, Mark put his arm around her shoulders. "Bethanne, it doesn't work. How did Kris get back to Seattle? Ken's car was still in the driveway when Dad and I got there."

"She could have driven back here in her car and surprised him."

"Why didn't the deputy see her car?"

"Maybe he got here around seven, and they went out driving to talk over their fight, and she shot him and dragged him into the house and . . ."

The look on his face stopped her. She buried her face in his chest. "Another piece of the puzzle with no place to put it," she said.

The next morning, Bethanne wrapped a flowered silk scarf around her head to hide the bandage.

Definitely not me, she thought, frowning at the mirror.

At her mom's suggestion, she had decided to skip Ken's funeral but go to the cemetery for the burial.

"You can stand away from the crowd," her mom had said, "and no one will notice you."

Bethanne knew going was probably dumb, but she wanted to see that Kris and Kimmie were all right. For Kris, losing Ken had to be like the end of the world. Unless she shot him.

That's what you're going for, Bethanne thought suddenly. To see if she looks guilty.

And to see Kimmie.

Peri wanted to go, too. Despite Kris's shoplifting, Peri had always liked her. Bethanne picked up Peri and drove to Valley Cemetery at the edge of town.

It spread over one of the low foothills that bordered one end of Valley. Driving through the iron gates, Bethanne gazed out over the sun-brightened expanse. Ancient trees as well as headstones—angels, lions—dotted it. All measures of time passing. Valley's founding families had sections in the cemetery toward the top of the hill. On the gravestones in the Taylor section, Bethanne could trace back her family to her great-grandparents. From where she was, she could see the century-old Douglas fir that sheltered her grandmother Beth's grave.

Someday, she might even be buried in Valley Cemetery. Her children and grandchildren would come visit her grave. As always, being there made her realize what a part she was in the wholeness of it all.

She continued to the newer section where Ken's grave would be, parking on the road by that area. The air smelled of freshly cut grass. In the distance, the sound of a lawn mower rumbled. A few butterflies flitted, drawn by the bright flowers left on the graves.

She and Peri sat on headstones, waiting until Ken's funeral procession arrived. They stayed well behind as the thirty or forty mourners moved to an open grave. Among the crowd, Bethanne saw the mayor, Dot's father, Dan Reid in his formal police uniform. Kris, dressed in black, stood with Kimmie near the grave. Kimmie's hair shone like spun gold in the sunshine. She wore the ruffly pink dress Bethanne had last seen her in.

Her best dress for her dad's funeral, Bethanne thought. Tears sprang to her eyes.

A black veil hid Kris's face. Her head was bent, looking toward the ground. Kimmie looked around, her face serious.

Bethanne stepped behind Peri to avoid Kimmie's gaze. She was too late. Kimmie's face brightened. She slipped from her mother's side, squeezing around the legs of the mourners. Kris turned her head, then gave a quick wave to Peri.

Kris thinks Kimmie's coming to Peri, Bethanne realized.

Crouching to greet Kimmie, Bethanne put a finger over her lips to show her to speak quietly. Kimmie threw her arms around her.

"I miss you," Kimmie whispered.

Kris must not have told her about me, Bethanne thought.

Tears filled her eyes again. "I'm sorry about your daddy."

Kimmie stepped back. She patted Bethanne on the shoulder. "Don't worry, Bethanne. Mama says we'll be a family again soon." Her head moved up and down.

What could Kris mean by that?

Kimmie took Bethanne's hand. "We're moving far away. Mama says it's a secret. You won't tell, will you, Bethanne?"

Bethanne wrestled with an answer. She didn't want to lie to Kimmie, but what if this news turned out to be important?

"Not if I don't have to," Bethanne said.

Kimmie nodded, as if she understood.

Probably does, Bethanne thought. Little girls can't always keep their secrets either.

"I have to learn a new language," Kimmie said. "Like this. Wee, wee. That means yes, yes." She giggled. "One boy at day care says that to go to the bathroom."

Oui was a French word. Why were they moving to France?

"Mama says I have to choose a new name, too. Any name I want." She swiveled her shoulders, rocking back and forth from foot to foot. "I don't want to change my name. But I might change it to Bethanne. It's my favorite name . . . except for Kimmie." She studied Bethanne. "Is that all right?"

144

"Kris is looking for her," Peri whispered.

Bethanne suddenly realized the minister had begun to speak.

She hugged Kimmie. "Go see your mom." When Kimmie reached Kris, Bethanne stood. "I'm going back to the car," she told Peri.

She needed to think about the things Kimmie had just told her.

In the car, she pulled from the glove compartment the paper with the list she'd made the day before. At the bottom she added, "Kris says the family will be together. In France?"

How could the family be together again if Ken is dead? Kris identified the body. Could she have lied? Yes, but the dental records confirmed her. Ken had perfect teeth. Like Birdman.

Bethanne took a sharp breath. Briefly, she saw Birdman saying to her mom, "Dad's a dentist in Seattle." He'd grinned. "Had to have perfect teeth."

Her chest tightened. What if they weren't burying Ken? What if Birdman lay in that coffin?

The thoughts spilled faster and faster. Ken kills Birdman and escapes to France before he's caught for embezzling Mrs. Talbot's money. Kris inherits four million dollars.

They did set me up, Bethanne thought, angry now.

She remembered the day she met Ken, how he'd said "She'll do very nicely." No wonder he gave her the creeps. He planned to kill her even then. And Birdman. They killed Birdman!

Had Kris hit her that night? How had she and Ken wrecked Birdman's truck? Bethanne shrugged. Those answers would come.

She looked out at the funeral group. It was

breaking up, people walking away. She jumped from the car. Dan Reid had just reached his.

Waving her paper, she raced to him. "Dan, Dan, I have something to tell you."

Thursday morning, Dan called Bethanne and her parents into the police station. They sat around his desk. One of the deputies brought in mugs of coffee for the adults and a can of Coke for Bethanne.

"The inquest has been postponed," Dan told them. "Kris Kirk's in a cell downstairs. I've had long talks with her trying to tie up the loose ends of this case."

"How is she?" Bethanne asked.

"Pretty depressed," he said, "but willing to talk about what happened. I don't think this whole scheme was her idea. I get the feeling that what her husband said went in that family."

Poor Kris, Bethanne thought. Maybe that's why she shoplifted. So she'd be caught and could get out of the situation. Now, it's too late. What will happen to her? And Kimmie?

"What about Kimmie? Bethanne asked.

"One of our women guards is watching out for her until we can decide what to do. Apparently, Kris has family in New York Kimmie can go to."

I'll never see her again. The thought hurt Bethanne as much as a physical blow.

"Kimmie must be so scared," Bethanne said.

Her dad scooted his chair closer to the desk. "I haven't got the whole thing straight. Was Birdman really the one who died that night?"

"Yeah," Dan said. "We looked at the body again. More closely. Found shrapnel in one leg. Birdman's dad said it was from a war injury. Medical records confirmed it."

"Poor guy," Bethanne's dad said.

Dan nodded. "The whole story goes back long before that night. It starts with the Kirks embezzling money from their clients. Ken Kirk figured they'd take as much as they could and leave the country. They set the date for the end of the summer. By then, they would have made off with a couple million, plus the life insurance."

He sipped his coffee and pushed the coffee mug away. "Tastes like they boiled this." He pushed a button on the telephone, and when a voice responded, said, "Bring three more Cokes.

"Then, Mrs. Talbot began to suspect something," Dan went on. "Ken knew they only had a couple weeks before she discovered what was going on. If they didn't act fast, they'd lose everything."

"That's where I come in," Bethanne said. She was drawing circles in the water drops on her soda can.

Dan nodded. "Ken was greedy. He'd taken out those life insurance policies over the past six months. I think he planned on using you from the beginning. You and Birdman."

"Poor Birdman," Bethanne's mom said.

"It doesn't seem fair," Bethanne said. "Birdman wrecks his life in the war, then gets killed by Ken Kirk." A scary thought hit her. "I didn't kill him, did I? I mean, those powder stains on my hands."

As Dan shook his head, a deputy came in with three cans of pop. He cleared away the coffee mugs.

When he'd left, Dan continued. "According to Kris, this is what happened. Ken kidnapped Birdman when he came to get the recyclables, a week before the Kirks went to Seattle. Ken hid the pickup in the garage. Either he forced Birdman to call his father, or Ken called him himself. He kept Birdman in the garage, drugged and tied up."

"You mean he was in there while I was working at the house?" Bethanne said. "I could have saved him?"

Her mom patted Bethanne's hand. "You couldn't have known."

That didn't make Bethanne feel any better.

"Ken set up the roses so we'd think Birdman was the Rosekiller and that he had run away." Dan shrugged. "Ken got the roses from the Rotary's Valentine dance. He and Kris were in charge of it."

He stood and paced the room while he continued to talk. "On Friday night, about seven, Ken returned to Valley. He went to the place you and Mark spotted Birdman's truck, Bethanne. Kris followed in her car. Leaving it off the road, they drove to their house. My deputy just happened to see Ken's car before Ken hid it in the garage. They cleaned away all signs of Birdman having been in there. Then Ken changed clothes with Birdman. Ken and Kris went into the house. You know what happened next."

"Kris knocked me out, right?"

Dan nodded. "Ken took the gun to the garage and shot Birdman."

"Oh," Bethanne said. The thought of Birdman's death rolled hard in her stomach.

"They carried Birdman into the house," Dan continued. "Ken held the gun in your hand and fired it. We went back to the house yesterday and found the bullet in the wall. Ken started the fire—not the lamp. He and Kris drove the pickup to where Kris's car was parked. After sending the truck over the cliff, they returned to Seattle in Kris's car. She dropped him off at another hotel. The next morning, he took a plane to New York. She was going to collect the life insurance, then meet him there before they all flew on to Paris."

"So where is Ken Kirk now?" Bethanne's dad asked.

"We've contacted the New York police," Dan said. "They'll get him." He sat back down at his desk. "That's about it. Next comes the trial. Since Kris is Ken's wife, she can't testify against him, but the information she's given us will make it easier for us to build the case. Her help should make her sentence shorter, too."

"She's a murderer," Bethanne's dad said.

"According to her," Dan told him, "Ken threatened to take their daughter away if she didn't help him."

"Poor woman," Bethanne's mom said.

"She chose her daughter over ours," Bethanne's dad argued. "She could have told someone what was going on and gotten help. Told Bethanne even. Kris saw her every day."

"Could I see Kris?" Bethanne asked. She

needed to confront her, find out why she let everything happen.

Nodding, Dan called in a policeman. He led Bethanne to a cool cement-walled room in the basement of the station. The area reeked of dampness, stale cigarette smoke, unwashed bodies. Bethanne sat behind a window. Kris sat on the other side. She had on a pale green cotton dress and soft slipperlike shoes. Her hair was uncombed, and her eyes were red and puffy. She wore no makeup.

They talked through a small hole. "I'm sorry, Bethanne," she said. Tears ran down her cheeks.

"Me, too," Bethanne told her. This was a woman who had everything: a beautiful little girl, career, home. A woman who helped her husband kill poor Birdman and left Bethanne to die. A woman who would have lived even better on the money they received. Oh, sure. Maybe those tears that day meant she'd tried to stop Ken. A phone call to the police was all it would have taken.

If you were her, afraid of losing Kimmie, overwhelmed by Ken, would you have had the strength?

To stop a murder? I hope so, Bethanne answered. She gazed at Kris. Her face showed so much pain. Okay, I'll give her my pity, but she's still guilty.

"I need to know," Bethanne said. "Why did Ken dress up like Birdman that night?"

"He put the rose at your house and followed you in Birdman's truck to make you think Birdman was stalking you. He said you'd tell people you saw Birdman in the house. They would think you imagined Ken was Birdman and shot him for that reason. That way you wouldn't be in so much trouble."

"But I could have died in the fire," Bethanne said, "so that wouldn't have mattered."

Kris looked down at her hands. "Ken promised to call the fire department when we left the house."

"Yeah," Bethanne said. "I sure believe that." Her anger made her hot, even in the cool room.

"It's true," Kris said, her eyes pleading. "Only when we drove away, he told me he changed his mind."

"Couldn't you have done anything?" Bethanne said.

Kris dropped her face in her hands and sobbed.

Bethanne sighed, feeling suddenly guilty. This was like kicking a sick cat. Ken was the one who deserved her anger.

"What about Kimmie?" Bethanne said quietly.

"They took her away. Bethanne, I know I'll go to jail. I deserve that. But losing Kimmie . . . the world might as well end." She looked directly at Bethanne. "I know how angry you are at me. Maybe you think I should lose her."

"No," Bethanne said.

"My sister and her husband in New York are taking her," Kris went on. "They've wanted children but never had them. The software firm they work for has a branch up in Ridge. They've asked for transfers. They'll keep Kimmie close so she can visit me." Her voice broke. Pausing, Kris wiped her eyes. "They'll be looking for a baby-sitter sometimes. How would you feel about doing that?"

Bethanne's heart leaped. She didn't want to lose Kimmie either. But what would Bethanne's mom and dad say about Bethanne's taking care of the child of the people who tried to murder her? child of the people who tried to murder her?

"I'll think about it," she told Kris.

24

She brought up baby-sitting Kimmie at dinner that night.

"Absolutely not," her father snapped. "Her parents tried to kill you."

"Kimmie had nothing to do with that," Bethanne said. "She's going to have a hard time—new family, new place to live. Maybe I can help her."

"It's like saying we forgive them," he grumbled.

"No, Daddy, it's like saying Kimmie is important no matter how bad her parents are. She needs to know that. Don't you see?" Bethanne looked to her mother, hoping for support.

"I agree with Bethanne," she said. "That little girl deserves more."

He sighed. "All right, but no baby-sitting at their house. We don't know these people. They may be nice, but they may be as bad as—"

Bethanne jumped up and hugged him. "Thanks, Daddy."

Boxer's bark underlined her relief.

A month later, Peri, Mark, and Bethanne sat around her patio table. Her mom came out, carrying the mail. She handed Bethanne a postcard with a picture of a Hawaiian beach.

Bethanne turned the card over and read, "We're

having a great time. Met two super guys from Seattle. Wish you were here. See you next week. Love, Dot and Lissa."

"How will the Football Four take that?" Peri asked, laughing.

"Bethanne," Kimmie called from the kitchen.

Bethanne was baby-sitting her that afternoon. Bethanne turned to see her hurrying from the house. Boxer, carrying his leash, trotted beside her.

"Boxer says he wants to go to the park," she said.

Bethanne checked her watch. Two-thirty. She didn't have to be at work at the restaurant until five.

While Mark snapped on the leash, she got the tennis ball, and they all walked to the neighborhood park. Bethanne showed Kimmie the blue and gray sign just erected at the park's entrance.

"Birdman Park," Bethanne read.

Tears stung her eyes. How would Kimmie feel someday when she learned what her parents had done to Birdman? She was seeing a counselor. He'd advised that for right now, Kimmie be told her parents went to jail for taking money that wasn't theirs. Later, she'd learn the whole truth. Hugging her now, Bethanne vowed to do everything she could to make her strong enough to handle the news.

Inside the entrance, they stopped at a newly installed vending machine. Pushing the button gave them a small bag of bird seed. When workmen had torn down Birdman's shack, they'd discovered thousands of dollars under the floor. His father had used the money to set up a fund to purchase food for the birds in the park.

Several children and parents played in the playground area, but no one sat around the fountain. Reaching it, Bethanne gave Kimmie the tennis ball. She, Peri, and Mark ran off to play with Boxer. Birds in the trees chirped over the fountain's burbling.

Bethanne sat on the bench. Suddenly, it seemed as though Birdman sat beside her. He smiled and touched his cap. As his image faded, she gazed at the small birds fluttering down. She poured bird seed into her hand and held it out.

She waited.